A MAGNOLIA ROW
NOVEL

Just a Number

ANNA MAY

JUST A NUMBER

A MAGNOLIA ROW NOVEL

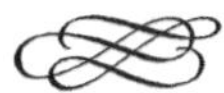

ANNA MAY

Rose House, LLC.

*In Loving Memory of
Lisa Luke Beasley*

MICAH

"Sugar," I hear from across the room, "why don't you take that sweater off? It's hotter than blue blazes in here."

I roll my eyes at my Nana, who is standing in her office door, hands on her hips. She's a little bitty thing, looking at me over her glasses as I dust the giant fountain at the center of our antique shop, a repurposed old church over a hundred years old. It's a beautiful, unique space, but the air conditioning functions about as well as a fish on a bicycle.

"Can we please go home?" I whine. "It's miserable in here and we're not going to have any customers anyway. As soon as they walk in and realize the air isn't working, they'll turn around and leave."

She shakes her head. "The sign says we're open until five, so we'll be here until five. Besides, I saw Pauline Cavendish when you took me to the bank this morning. She said she may stop by."

"All the more reason to close the store. You know she's crazier than a shithouse rat."

"Hush up with that vulgar mouth, Micah Bonaventure."

"Can we please to home?"

"No."

I sigh. If I didn't have to drive her home, I'd leave her here.

Nana eyed me and shook her head. "You and those godforsaken sweaters. You dress like more of a granny than me."

"My neckline suggests otherwise," I say, looking down at my cleavage. "Besides, it's my signature style. I have to stay on brand."

She chuckles and shakes her head. I got her with that one, which is rare.

I do have to admit I may be a little too fond of cardigans. I hate my arms, and sweaters cover them despite the heat. Since my job at our antique store is to merchandise and maintain the floorspace, I'm always moving, and every time I see a jiggle out of the corner of my eye or get a glimpse of it in one of the old mirrors we have for sale, I cringe. They make me look twice the size I already am. When a customer comes in, I feel like they're staring at my flab. I simply feel better if they're covered.

And my legs. My legs are just as bad.

"Once you finish cleaning," Nana says, giving up on trying to get me to remove my sweater, "take some more pictures for the insta-thing on your phone," she says. "We always get inquiries after you post something."

"Yes, ma'am," I say, exasperated as I wipe sweat from my forehead. There's no sense in arguing.

She goes back to her desk, and I finish dusting an antique chifforobe that's been here for ages. It's a beautiful piece, made of oak with an irregular and vibrant wood grain. I've contemplated taking it home on more than one occasion, but Nana and I don't have space for it in the small house we share.

Once I'm done, I take out a rag and ladder to clean the color block stained-glass windows. This feature is my favorite part of this old space. The panes are thin enough to let in plenty of light, which casts hues of pink, orange, and green onto the floor of the shop. The glass is rippled and I love the distortion it casts on the world outside, like it's all a dream.

After the whole store is dusted and polished, I take a few photos to post on our social media accounts. Nana is right about one thing—once I gave the store an online presence, business more than tripled. Now we get clients from all over the South looking for heavy, ornate dining room sets, bed frames, or paintings and pottery we've snagged from local estate sales. Our small town of Magnolia Row, Alabama, has enough old houses, not to mention old money, to supply us with a steady stream of inventory. At least once a year, some elderly rich person dies and we end up with more items than we can handle.

But the one thing that never sells, and will probably still be here once I'm gone, is the fountain. It sits in the middle of our floorspace as the most unique and elaborate piece we carry. Nana purchased it for a fraction of what it's worth when the Florablanca Inn went bankrupt years before I was born. It was originally in the lobby of the hotel and features three scantily-clad sirens—with magnolias in their hair and strategically covering their bodies—as the center pillar. Water is supposed to come from their mouths into the trough below, but it hasn't functioned since it was housed in the hotel. It's Nana's favorite piece, and she priced it so high I doubt anyone will ever buy it.

I place a few satin flowers in the lap of one of the sirens to add a pop of color to my photo, then take a few shots from different angles until I have one good enough to post.

I walk back to Nana's office to get a rubber band for a ponytail and catch Nana putting four sugar packets in her glass of iced tea.

"Nana!" I say, running to the desk and snatching them out of her hand. "You know you can't have this!"

"That's not sugar," she says, stirring her tea.

"It is!" I say, staring at her like I'm shocked, even though I'm not. Nana's a diabetic and has heart disease. To top it off, she's terrible at keeping up with her medication and diet. Her addiction to sweet tea and fried food has been a struggle. She either eats and doesn't take her medicine, or she takes her medicine and doesn't eat. Her blood sugar is all over the place. "I can read," I continue, pointing at the little paper packet. "Pure cane sugar."

"It doesn't say that."

"Stop trying to gaslight me."

She takes a sip. "Not sweet at all."

I shake my head. "Nana. Dr. Denbigh says you have to take care of yourself. You can't—"

She makes a gesture as if to shoo me away. "I have crowns in my teeth older than that kid."

"He went to medical school."

She doesn't respond, but goes back to updating the inventory spreadsheet and drinking her sweet tea like I'm not there. I walk behind the desk and open the top drawer.

I'm looking for a rubber band, but instead find a whole box of sugar. Nana cuts her eyes at me. I simply remove the box, dig for a rubber band, and walk to the bathroom to fix my hair, chucking the box of sugar in the trash after dousing it with water.

I swear I sprout more gray hair every time I catch her with sugar or something fried. I'm thirty years old. At this rate, I'll be completely white-haired by the time I'm forty. When people ask why I don't want kids, I tell them it's because I'm too busy raising my nana.

As I'm walking back into the cramped office, my cell phone dings. It's Garrett, wanting to know if I can come over tomorrow night.

"Who's texting you?" Nana asks.

"No one," I say without looking at her.

She shakes her head. "Who's gaslighting now?"

I roll my eyes and ignore her comment.

Garrett is my undefined boyfriend, or "situation-ship," as my friend Patsy calls it. We met online a year ago, and he lives about an hour and a half away, in Montgomery. He owns some kind of computer programming company. I don't pretend to understand what exactly he does, but he has a crazy schedule and doesn't have a lot of time for dating or commitments. He calls it being married to his career, which I totally understand. Since he's always busy, we agreed to keep our relationship casual. Maybe one day it'll be something more, but for now I'm enjoying it for what it is.

Neither Nana nor any of my friends like him or our relationship, but it's not like I have guys banging down my door. I'm not the girl who's ever been able to easily get a boyfriend. I've always been bigger, both in height and weight, and it makes me awkward. The fact that a guy like Garrett wants to spend any time with me at all is a miracle in and of itself. Patsy is constantly telling me I'm wasting my time, but it's not like I'm in a hurry to have kids and settle down. Patsy has a big family with a lot of kids, but that's just not me. I would like to have a great romance at some point, but for now, Nana and I have each other, like we always have, and it's enough.

I respond to Garrett and tell him I'd love to come see him, then spend the rest of the day planning my outfit in my head. Once it's finally time to close, I drive Nana to the home we share. Neither of us mention Garrett again.

RHODES

When I got the call about a potential job restoring an old hotel in Magnolia Row, I jumped. I'd never been to the small Alabama town, but I'd heard all about it when I was in architecture school. It's known for its stunning historic homes, manicured lawns, and picturesque location on the Florablanca River. It sounds like a dream.

The hotel I was contacted about was once a hotspot for Southern travelers, particularly honeymooners, but for the past thirty years has been completely ignored and unoccupied. The new owner reached out to me for a proposal to overhaul the hotel and completely restore it to its original grandeur.

It's the day of my first meeting with the potential client, and I make the three-hour drive south from my loft in Birmingham. It's all interstate until Montgomery, then I have an hour and a half of rural roads lined with cow pastures, oaks full of Spanish moss, and the occasional old farmhouse set back from the road like a totem to the past. It's a beautiful day despite the heat, and I'm glad to be out of the congested city.

I drive into Magnolia Row and am immediately transported back in time. It's quaint, as I thought it would be, and exquisite. Passing through the historic district, I see every kind of architecture I would expect from a town that boomed in the late 1800s. Victorian, Italianate, and Greek revival houses line the streets. Even the trees are immaculate – the most gorgeous oaks, magnolias, and dogwoods complement each house. The homes themselves are circled with azaleas and hydrangeas that no doubt give a spray of wild, bright colors in the spring.

Now I'm even more hungry to get this job. It'll give me an excuse to come back and see the town through all the seasons.

I'm early, so I stop at a coffee shop on Main Street to get an iced latte. This stretch of road is the beating heart of town, and is even more vibrant than the residential streets. Instead of oaks, this street is lined with massive magnolia trees. If it weren't for the modern cars, I'd swear I'd somehow been transported back to the 1950s. I can't believe how well preserved the whole area is.

As soon as I step out of my car, I regret wearing a suit instead of something more casual and cool to meet the investor who purchased the hotel. My clothes feel like an oven. Luckily, the air conditioning in the coffee shop is on full blast. The girl behind the counter takes my order and asks me where I'm from. She's short, with dirty blonde hair and a pink apron.

"Birmingham," I tell her, strumming my thumbs along the counter and taking in my quaint surroundings. "I'm an architect and have a meeting with the new owner of Florablanca Inn."

"Wow!" she says, running my card for my iced coffee. "I can't believe someone actually wants to throw money into that old thing."

"I haven't seen it yet," I tell her. "Is it in bad shape?"

She makes a hard-to-read face and steps behind the barista counter to make my drink. "I'm told it used to be beautiful," she says, "but I've only ever known it as a creepy bat shack. A lot of the houses in the Victorian Village are in rough shape. It's Magnolia Row's dirty little dilapidated secret."

I raise my eyebrows and chuckle. "Why is that? The rest of the town is so stunning."

"I'm not really sure. Something about a fire on Old Vic Road a long time ago. The hotel is the first thing you'll see. If you keep going down that street, you'll be able to see where it was full of Victorian houses a hundred years ago. Most of them are gone now. There's a house about a mile from the hotel in similar shape. My friends and I used break into it when we were bored in high school."

"That sounds fun!" I say, but she merely shrugs and finishes making my coffee.

"Good luck to you," she says, handing it to me. "I hope you enjoy a challenge."

"I do," I say, almost as a reminder to myself.

I sit in a corner table to drink my coffee, which is better

than I'd expected. Once I'm done, I wave goodbye to the barista and drive a few blocks over to the hotel.

The girl at the coffee shop was right. This road isn't as well-kept as the main drag, and the hotel stands as a testament to its neglect. I don't see any cars or signs of life near the building, so I park, grab my camera, laser distance meter, pen, and notepad and help myself to a walk around the exterior.

It isn't easy. The yard is overgrown with weeds and I'm cognizant of the fact that I could step on a snake at any moment. I also note the back of the hotel overlooks the river, which makes me even more anxious about cottonmouths.

I take a few photos. The building is a four story, L-shaped Victorian with six stacks of bay box windows. The lobby entrance on the front corner is at an angle. It still has the original turned spandrils and sawn balusters on the long porches that span each wing on the front. It's a stunning building, and I've never seen anything quite like it. Even though the paint is peeling off, kudzu is growing over parts, and spiderwebs glisten in the sun, I can perfectly imagine what this place looked like in its prime.

God, I hope I get this job.

In the back, what was once an impressive courtyard is tucked into the corner of the L-shaped building. The original tile on the patio is visible, but the earth is well on its way to reclaiming it under dark green growth. Broken concrete furniture and statues dot the lawn, and I take few photos to later see if I can find replacements of something similar, assuming I get the job.

"Hi!" I hear from behind me, and I'm so startled I almost drop my camera.

I turn to see a tall woman in a skin-tight black dress and heels. She's dark-complected and has long black hair and red pointy nails. She's struggling to walk towards me in her completely inappropriate stilettos.

I wave to her. "I'll come to you," I say, navigating my way off the patio and towards the corner of the building where she's waiting. She's older than I'd thought she'd be, though she's doing her best to look younger. From far away, I would've guessed she's close to my own age of forty-five, but as I get closer, I see she easily has fifteen to twenty years on me.

"I'm Wilhelmina Caxton," she says, holding out her hand.

I return the gesture. "Rhodes Cauley."

"Well, aren't you a tall drink o' water?" She takes her sunglasses off and looks me up and down. Her eyes are lined with a thick layer of black make-up that somehow hasn't smudged despite the sweat breaking out on her face.

"Thank you," I say, looking to the ground and shuffling my feet, unsure what to say.

"So, what do you think?" she said, dramatically holding out her hands.

"It's a gorgeous building. I need to go inside to assess everything, but it looks like there's a lot here to work with. I'm delighted to be considered for the project."

To be honest, I'm more than delighted. I'm ecstatic. When I quit my job at the largest architecture firm in Birmingham last year, I opened up my own business to focus solely on historic restoration and preservation. I was so tired of designing new, boring commercial spaces. Old buildings are more beautiful, more challenging, and more rewarding. This hotel is everything I'd hoped it'd be, and I'm a little overwhelmed by the prospect of finally bidding on my dream job after twenty years in the profession.

She smiles and pats me on the shoulder, then leads me inside, walking carefully with short steps.

"I have a passion for old, neglected things, Mr. Cauley, being an old, neglected thing myself." She leads me into the lobby and, for a moment, I forget to maintain an air of professionalism. My mouth drops open at the sheer scale of this place. "May I call you Rhodes?" she asks, bringing me back to reality.

"Rhodes is fine," I say, clearing my throat.

She rubs my arm. "As you can see, this hotel was once the jewel of this town," she says. She's right. The lobby is massive with rough marble floors. The ceiling looks to be about twenty feet high, and there's a spot in the center which once held what was probably an impressive and very expensive chandelier. There's ample room for seating and lounging, and in the back are French doors—with broken glass—leading to the courtyard.

"Once we're done, I want this place to be not only the jewel of Magnolia Row, but the jewel of the whole state of Alabama. I want it shiny, restored, and even more glamorous than it was before. I have a decorator who wants to do every room in a different color and theme, but first we need to work on the bones. That's your job. We're sparing no expense, darling. You just tell me what you need and whom to pay."

I'm a little confused. I'd thought I was here to get a lay of the land so I could write up a proposal. I assumed I'd be bidding against other architects. "I have the job?"

"Of course," she said. "I wouldn't bring you all the way down here for nothing."

I'm shocked. I expected a much more difficult process. "Wow. Thank you for the opportunity, Ms. Caxton."

"It's Mrs. Caxton. My husband is dead, but I still like the sound of the 'Mrs.' It adds a bit of class, don't you think?"

I raise my eyebrows. "Yes" seems to be the correct answer here, so I agree.

We walk down the hall of the south wing. I'm struggling to take it all in and keep up with her conversation.

"My late husband left me with four horrid stepchildren and more money than I know what to do with. I intend to waste as much of it as possible before I die. Like I said, I simply adore these old buildings. When I heard about this place, I had to have it."

"You aren't from here?" I ask, ducking under a partially fallen beam.

"No, honey. I'm from Fairhope, but my daddy used to bring me here as a child. He was in food distribution and had business with the peanut farmers around these parts."

"And your husband?" It's not my business, but I can't help asking.

"A professional scoundrel," she says with a loud, throaty laugh. "But he was rich, which is really what matters."

I smile and nod. "Apparently so."

"Darling, what do you need from me right now?"

"I'd like to explore a little bit, get some photos and measurements, then take all of this back home and come up with some numbers for you. Do you know if the city has any of the original plans?"

"The little real estate man said something about it, but I didn't get them."

"That's fine. I'll swing by and see what they have."

"Wonderful, darling. If you have any trouble, you call me."

"I will."

She disappears down the long, dusty corridor and stands by her car, talking on the phone, while I take extensive photos and measurements of the exterior and interior. An area of the south wing has a lot of decay. It will have to be completely ripped out, but on the whole, I'm pleasantly surprised at how well the building has stood up to decades of neglect. Even when I go upstairs, the carpet is rotten but the boards beneath my feet don't give way as much as I expect. Most of the windows have been boarded up, which kept the rain out after the glass shattered or was removed, but that's an easy fix. I'm not able to get onto the tiled roof, but considering how well the structure has held up, I'm betting the roof is in pretty good shape.

I have some coveralls in my SUV, so I go outside, remove my jacket, and put those on over my dress pants and button-down shirt, then shimmy under the hotel, carefully dodging spiders. The foundation is made of massive wooden beams that show typical signs of age, but are relatively solid, with the exception of the problem area in the south wing.

I brush myself off after I crawl out and approach Mrs. Caxton, who is watching me and smoking by her car.

"Well?" she asks, smiling.

"I'm quite pleased," I say. "There are a few trouble spots, but nothing that can't be fixed. Is there a specific contractor you're interested in?"

"No, darling. I figured I'd let you handle that." She reaches forward and brushes cobwebs out of my hair. It's a strangely intimate gesture and makes me a little uncomfortable.

"What kind of budget do you have in mind?" I ask, clearing my throat.

"Don't you worry about money."

I stand there for a moment with my mouth open. I'm stunned this woman is handing this project to me sight unseen. I'm stunned she doesn't have a budget. I'm stunned she's flicking cigarette ashes into a pile of dry, dead underbrush that could light this place up in seconds.

"Do you mind asking how you decided on me as your architect?" I ask. "Have you seen my work, or did someone refer you?"

"I looked you up on the Google."

I pause, staring at her with what I know must be a dumbfounded expression. "That's it?"

"Well, I liked your picture. You're handsome, and you have an honest face."

I have no idea how to respond. I have no doubt I'll do a phenomenal job, but she literally knows nothing about me.

"You need to work on your poker face, Rhodes." She laughs again with a hearty, deep voice. "My instincts have never failed me. You're the right man for the job."

"Thank you. I'm thrilled to be a part of it."

"When do you go back to Birmingham?" she asks before taking a long drag from her cigarette.

"Saturday. I thought I'd stay a few days to get a feel for the town and find out as much as I can about the hotel."

"How about you and I go down to that little steakhouse for dinner?"

This…is awkward. There's no way I'm letting this relationship be anything other than business, despite how hungry I am for this project.

"I'd like to get started on my proposal and make some phone calls, if you don't mind." I look at my watch. "If I hurry, I should be able to get to the courthouse today."

"Of course," she says, not hiding her disappointment. "Send me what you have when you have it. I'm looking forward to working with you."

"Yes, ma'am."

She winks at me, then gets in her car—an Aston Martin.

I feel like I've entered a different world. I can't believe this is my life.

*A*t the courthouse, I'm thrilled the city has copies of all of the original paperwork on the hotel, down to the blueprints and original permits. I make copies of everything.

"Is it true some rich lady from Mobile bought the hotel?" the girl at the desk asks me.

"Fairhope, actually. And yes. I'm the architect she hired."

She smiles. "You're not from here." She says it as a statement more than a question.

"No, ma'am. I'm from Birmingham."

"You know," she says, "the Finnegan House is a museum now. It's in the historic district. They have a whole mess of old photos you can look at. I bet there's some of the hotel."

"That'd be great! Are they open?"

"They're probably closed for the day, but if you're still here tomorrow, you should swing by. My aunt runs it."

"I'll do that," I say. "Thank you!"

I take my copies and go back to my hotel after picking up some barbeque take-out for dinner. And a t-shirt. I can't go to Big Ol' Butts BBQ and not get a t-shirt.

I spend the rest of the night going through my pictures. I have so many ideas my head is spinning, and I have the perfect contractor to help me with the project. I work until almost three in the morning, and when my head hits the pillow, I dream about the Florablanca Inn.

The next morning, I go to Finnegan House as soon as it opens. It's a massive white Greek revival with Corinthian columns in the heart of Magnolia Row.

I'm greeted by an older lady wearing flowing dark pink pants with a matching cardigan over a black shirt. She's wearing gaudy costume jewelry, rings on every finger, and so many necklaces she jingles when she walks. Her hair is short, straight, and gray, and she carries herself like a queen.

This place is spectacular. It has floor-length windows and a porch that wraps around the entire house. It's decorated immaculately in rich greens, blues, and yellows. I can only imagine what kind of decadent parties were once held here.

"Ruth Cottar," the lady says, holding out her hand when I walk in. "I don't know you."

"No, I'm not from here," I say, shaking her hand. She looks me over, never cracking a smile. "I'm the architect overseeing the restoration of the Florablanca Inn."

"Ah," she says, softening a bit. "Well, I'm glad something is being done about it. It's been a blight on this town. All these beautiful houses, yet that old dump was left to rot."

I'm surprised to hear it referred to as a dump, as I see nothing but potential. But to each their own, I guess.

"I was told you have some old photos of the building."

"Yes, we do." She stands there for a beat and doesn't move.

"May I see them?" I ask.

"Of course." She leads me up the stairs. "Did you want the formal tour of the house or just the photos?"

"Just the photos for now, but I'll probably come back for the tour on another visit. This house is beautiful."

"Yes, it is."

The old wooden floorboards creak beneath our feet despite the heavy rugs. She leads me to what was once a bedroom on the north side, which is now lined with display cases on all walls and one in the center. Dozens and dozens of black and white photographs are framed with little description cards. In the back corner, near the old fireplace, she slides back the glass and takes out an album.

"The original owner of the hotel took these the first year it was open," she says.

I'm so excited my heart skips a beat as I look through it. Page after page of hotel images are included, along with smiling faces in Edwardian garb. There's even a clear shot of the lobby taken from the entrance of the front door, showcasing a fountain with a trio of sirens wearing nothing but magnolia flowers, shooting water from their mouths. I've never seen anything like it.

"This is a gold mine," I say.

"Take it," she says, "if you think it will help."

"Are you sure?"

"Of course, as long as you promise to return everything when you're finished."

"Absolutely."

"Is there anything else I can do to help?"

"No. I'd like to look around for a bit, if you don't mind. Kind of get a feel for the town's history and character. You have a lot of great stuff here."

"I'll be downstairs if you need anything," she says, folding her hands and showing herself out.

I spend another two hours flipping through the hotel album and looking at all the photos and antiques in the house. The town has a rich history going back to the 1870s, when it boomed with merchants due to the river and a railroad that ran from Mobile to Montgomery. It was one of the only prosperous areas in this part of Alabama during Reconstruction.

I go back downstairs and find Ms. Cottar on a settee, staring out the window at the passing cars. I clear my throat to get her attention. She stands and meets me in the foyer.

"Is that all you need?" she asks.

"Yes, for now, though I do have a question." She nods. "Do you know what happened to the contents of the hotel? The furniture, the decor? There's a beautiful fountain in one of the photos."

"Well, everything was auctioned off. In fact, we have two of the bedroom suites upstairs, and some of the furniture you see in these sitting rooms is from the ballroom, though they have been reupholstered, of course. So I guess the answer is everywhere. Everyone in town seems to have gotten a piece of the hotel before it was shuttered. Though you mentioned the fountain. I believe Barbara Bonaventure has it at her store."

"Her store? Where is that?"

"Bonaventure Antiques. Drive north down this very road out of the historic district. It'll be on your left. It's in an old church."

"Thank you. I'll go there now."

An antique store in an old church. I should've guessed.

It's Friday, and all I can think about is seeing Garrett tonight. My best friend, Sistine, asked me to hang out at Cattywampus Brewing for a girls' night with our friend Kendall, but since Garrett finally has some free time, I need to take advantage of it. Besides, I can see my girlfriends anytime.

I'll have to go home and shower after being in this hot-as-Hades store all day, but that's okay. Garrett usually works late, so I'll have plenty of time to primp.

"Do you have any plans tonight?" Nana asks as we eat lunch in her office.

"I may drive up to Montgomery." She knows what this means without me telling her who I'm meeting. She gives me a look but doesn't say anything, and we finish lunch in silence.

I spend most of the day taking pictures to post on social media next week. Last month, a man drove all the way from New Orleans to buy an old steamer trunk. I seem to have a knack for online marketing, and it's something I enjoy. I love every piece we have in the store, having hand-picked them all myself with Nana, and it's nice to show them off and help them find new homes to add to their history.

The sun is finally dipping below the tops of the pine trees outside, signaling it's almost time to close up shop. I'm in the back office with Nana, arguing over the price of a set of lamps, when the bell of the front door jingles.

I pull my cardigan closed and walk out to the floor of the store, which was once the sanctuary of the church, and see a tall, handsome man with wide, light blue eyes looking around the space as if in awe.

"Hi," I say, navigating the crowded floorspace to where he stands. "Welcome to Bonaventure Antiques."

"Hello," he says, finally noticing me as I approach. He smiles, and for a moment we lock eyes in silence. He's gorgeous—drop dead, take-me-now gorgeous. He's taller than me, lean, and has broad shoulders and salt-and-pepper curtain hair. His face is chiseled, with high cheekbones and a firm, square jawline. "Is there something I can help you with?" I muster, my voice cracking.

"Maybe. I heard you have—" He stops mid-sentence and his face lights up. "Yes, you do."

"What?" I ask, following his line of sight. The fountain has caught his attention. He walks over to it and I follow, my heels clacking on the old wooden floor.

"It's beautiful," he said, reaching out to touch it as if mesmerized.

"Yes," I say, a little confused. "It's my favorite thing in the store. Did you see it on our Insta, or—"

"No, in a photo of the old hotel."

"Oh, yeah! The Florablanca."

"That's the one! I've been hired to oversee the restoration." He finally takes his focus off the fountain and looks at me. He pauses and stares.

"What?" I ask awkwardly.

"You, uh, your hair. It's quite vibrant."

"Oh, um, thanks. I grew it myself." I nervously grab a strand that fell in front of my shoulder and play with it, unsure of what to do with my hands. People have always commented on my hair. It's bright honking orange. When I was little, I hated it. Now, I thank the Lord it's bold enough for me to not have to spend a fortune on hair dye to keep it up.

"Hello," Nana says from behind me. I jump. I hadn't realized she was there.

"Hi, I'm Rhodes," he says, properly introducing himself. "I'm the architect overseeing the restoration of Florablanca Inn."

"Oh, how wonderful! I'm Barbara Bonaventure, and this is my granddaughter, Micah."

"It's nice to meet you both." His bright eyes wander the room as if he's mesmerized. "This space is incredible!"

"Thank you." Nana is all politeness, though there's a mischievous twinkle in her eye. "Micah, why don't you show him around? I'll be in the office if you need anything." She winks at me, pushes me towards him, and leaves us alone in the sanctuary.

Rhodes returns his attention to the fountain. "Does it still work?" he asks.

"I have no idea. Nana wasn't sure if the floor could support the weight, so we never put water in it." I wring my hands and notice that my palms are sweaty, and I don't think it's just the heat.

"How long have y'all been here?"

"We got here around nine this morning."

"No, I mean, the store…"

Of course. I'm such an idiot. I don't know why I'm suddenly nervous.

"Right. Sorry." I feel my face flush. "Nana bought the place before I was born. It was Magnolia Row Baptist Church for a long time and, from what I'm told, it had a large congregation until the preacher, um…" I hesitate. It's a morbid story, but Rhodes raises his eyebrows like he wants me to continue. "The preacher shot his wife in the rectory." I blurt out. No point in sugarcoating. It's a wild story.

Rhodes looks at me, bewildered.

"Yeah, the church closed after that. Nothing turns folks off religion like murder. Nana got the building for cheap, and we use the rectory for storage."

"Wow! Um, okay." He runs his fingers through his hair and has a baffled look on his face. "Well, it's the perfect place for an antique store. You have some beautiful pieces."

He starts to meander, walking alongside the old church pews against the wall. In the back, he spots an upright antique piano with painted roses on the sides. "I love this," he says, emphasizing the word 'love.'

"We got it at an estate sale in town."

"Is that where most of your items come from?"

"For the most part, yes. Locally, people usually give us first stab at their collections. We used to go all over the South. Not so much anymore since Nana's gotten older, but every now and then we'll go to Montgomery or Mobile to pick up something."

"What's your favorite piece?" he asks.

I show him an art nouveau buffet table on the opposite wall. It has green marble tile on the top and is made of gnarled cherry wood.

"Incredible," he says, kneeling and running his hands up and down the legs. I pause for a minute and focus on how long his fingers are, how gingerly he caresses the wood, and for a brief second I allow myself to imagine it's my legs he's touching.

No, no, no, I tell myself, trying to clear my head. *I do not need a crush right now. I have a guy waiting for me in Montgomery I'm seeing tonight. The last thing I need is for this handsome stranger to distract me. But my God, he's sexy.*

"What's this one's story?" he asks, his hands still on the wood.

"Nana got that in Mobile when I was little. We think it dates to the 1910s. Apparently, it was originally owned by a madam at a high-class whorehouse in New Orleans, though I don't think we have reliable provenance. Makes for a great story, though. I like to imagine her keeping a ledger of clients in the drawers."

Rhodes stands up and moves his hands along the tiles.

He's so tactile, like he's trying to channel the energy of each piece when he touches it. Most people simply come in and look around. Rhodes wants to touch everything, as if he won't truly see it unless he lays his hands on it.

"That's a great story. I kinda want to buy this for my condo."

"Oh, you live at the beach?"

"No, downtown Birmingham. They converted the old City Federal building into condos and I bought one after my divorce."

So, he's single…maybe.

Ugh. I need to stop. He probably has a thin, stunning girlfriend who drinks cosmopolitans on the roof of his building overlooking the glittery city.

And I have Garrett. Kind of. In a noncommittal way.

"I could stay in here all day," he says, looking at a painting between two of the stained-glass windows.

"Well, we're closing soon," I say, remembering I need to get home and shower before making the drive to Montgomery.

Nana pops her head out of the office. "We can stay open late if you want us to," she says. I should've known she was eavesdropping.

"No, it's fine. I have work to do. Do you mind if I ask how much you want for the fountain? My client would be very interested in seeing this restored to the hotel, and I'd love to incorporate it into my design. We're trying to return it as close to its former glory as possible."

"I'll work something up for you," says Nana, though I'm

sure it'll break her heart to part with it. She walks towards us.

"Thank you. I'll stop by next time I'm in town. For now, I'll get out of your hair. It was nice to meet you, Ms. Bonaventure. And you too, Micah."

The sound of my name coming out of his mouth sends chills down my spine.

"It was nice to meet you too, Rhodes," called Nana. "Don't been a stranger."

"I won't." He smiles at me, then turns and leaves, the closing of the door echoing through the quiet space.

Nana pokes me in the side. "Oh, Micah. That man made me want to lose my religion. Have you ever seen someone so handsome?"

"Nana, he's too young for you."

"But not for you. He wasn't wearing a ring."

I hate to admit I did notice. "He probably has a girlfriend."

"You could change that."

"Nana! I'm not going after some architect who doesn't even live here. Besides, I have Garrett."

"Who also does not live here."

"Garrett's closer than Birmingham."

"Micah, I'm just saying. If this Rhodes fella's gonna be in Magnolia Row working on the hotel, maybe give him some of your time. He looks like someone worth knowing."

I sigh heavily and shoot her a look, letting her know I am done with this conversation. "Are you ready to go?"

"I reckon," she says, shaking her head.

She walks into the office, leaving me alone in the store. The air seems to have shifted, like Rhodes walked in and charged the energy in all these old beautiful items. Now he haunts the space, and I'm standing in his wake.

I leave the antique shop in a daze. The store itself was beyond all my wildest expectations. Every piece is valuable, unique, and carefully curated. And Micah...

Micah is the most beautiful woman I've ever seen. She's tall, probably five ten if I'm guessing correctly. I can actually talk to her without stooping down. She has a wild mane of bright red hair, smooth skin, and the most vibrant emerald eyes. When she was showing me the art nouveau buffet table, all I could think about was how the color in the green tile matched the colors in her irises. No wonder it's her favorite piece. She has great taste. Apart from the fountain, that table is probably the most expensive thing in the store.

She looks young, probably too young for me, but I'm a terrible judge of age. Besides, I haven't dated in over twenty years, so I wouldn't even know where to start. She wasn't wearing a ring. I did note that.

Everything about this town has me buzzing. I decide to stay one more night and drive back to Birmingham tomorrow. Once I get back to my hotel, I'll send a few emails, then take a walk downtown to get a better feel for the place.

Maybe I'll run into Micah.

She'll probably be out with a boyfriend or partner or someone who lives here and has known her for her entire life. Someone I can't compete with.

But maybe not, since she wasn't wearing a ring. I hold onto that thread like a kid holding a balloon string.

This is strange. I haven't had a crush since my ex-wife, before we were married and in college. I forgot how quick it happens, how it takes over your entire mood and train of thought. I'm way too old for this. I'm forty-five, not twenty.

Once I get to my room I shower, email a friend in Atlanta who may know how to get the fountain up and running, send a note to Mrs. Caxton to let her know I found the fountain, and reach out to a contractor acquaintance in Savannah who specializes in old building restoration. Hopefully he can help me find the right workers for this project.

I'm so excited I feel high. I've never done drugs in my life, but I think this is probably how it feels. Everything is beautiful and there's nothing but good things to come. This is exactly the kind of project I dreamt of when I started my own firm, and it landed in my lap with very little effort on my part. I'm the luckiest man in the world.

I leave the hotel wearing a blue polo, jeans, and boat

shoes. With a spring in my step, I head downtown. I decide to grab a bite to eat at the little barbeque joint again and think about checking out the local brewery on the river. Maybe I'll meet some locals who can tell me stories about the hotel. I make a mental note to put an ad in the paper and on social media for stories about the building. Maybe we can incorporate them into a publicity campaign.

I shake my head. PR is beyond the scope of what I was hired to do. I'm so excited to be working on this project I can't help myself. I feel like a kid again.

When I get downtown, I have trouble finding a parking spot. For such a tiny town, Magnolia Row seems to have a decent nightlife. Once I find a place to leave the car, I make my way past a few teenagers in Magnolia Row High School t-shirts and follow my nose for food. The entire town smells like smoked meat and my stomach is roaring. I scan the faces I pass but don't see anyone familiar.

But honestly, there's really only one I'm looking for.

MICAH

After we close the store, I drive my grandmother to the home we share on the other side of town. She talks about the architect the entire way.

"I'm just saying," she says. "He was a tall glass of water if I've ever seen one. Honey, if I were your age—"

"Nana, please stop!" I shake my head and try to pay attention to the road.

"I'd sink my claws into him and not let go. He's got a calm, debonair way about him, like Cary Grant or Robert Redford. Like he stepped out of Old Hollywood, you know?"

All I can do is shake my head, but she keeps going.

"Honey, a man like that will kiss you like it's a sin, then hold you all night to protect you."

"Nana—"

"He'll buy you nice jewelry, put you up in a fancy house, and then when the lights go out—"

"Okay, that's enough. I don't want to talk about the architect anymore."

"He'd be better than what's-his-name in Montgomery."

"Garrett. You know his name."

"I'm trying to forget. Rhodes is a much nicer name. Sounds like royalty. Lord Rhodes of Magnolia Row."

I shake my head. "You've been watching too much *Bridgerton*."

I pull into the driveway. Our house is small, modest, and smells like my grandmother's perfume. I moved in with Nana after my mom skipped town when I was ten years old, so this has always been home to me. It may be dated and feel like a time capsule from the seventies, but I love it. It even has the original brown and orange shag carpet and puke-green enamel stove in the kitchen. Most people probably think it's tacky, but I would never change a thing.

Once we get inside, Nana assures me she has enough leftovers for dinner and waves me off so I can get ready for my not-really-a-date thing. I don't think it's a date, anyway. I'm hanging out with Garrett at his place after he gets off work. Nothing crazy.

I shower, washing the sticky sweat from my body after being in the hot store all day. Rhodes didn't help matters. I know I turned twenty shades of red every time he looked at me. It should be a crime to look that good. Nana's at least right about that.

I decide to wear my hair up tonight, even though it makes my face look extra round. August in Alabama is way too hot to have long, thick hair on your neck. I know I'll sweat most of it off, but I still wear a full face of makeup with my signature red lipstick and fake—but tasteful—lashes. I wear a pink floral maxi dress to cover my legs with a white shrug to hide my arms. The dress is low, so at least my ample cleavage is showing.

Garrett always says he likes chesty women, so I might as well flaunt it.

Once I'm ready, I check Nana's pill organizer and realize she hasn't taken her afternoon meds, so I fish them out and take them to her in the living room.

"I thought I took those."

"Apparently not."

"I guess I was thinking about yesterday." She shakes her head, then downs them with some (hopefully) unsweet iced tea.

"I love you, Nana."

"Love you too, sugar bug. Be careful on them roads."

"I will."

I get in my little blue hatchback, text Garrett to let him know I'm on my way, then put on a playlist of Kacey Musgraves and drive to Montgomery in the dark. The entire journey is on poorly lit backroads, and even though it's grossly hot outside, the deer are unseasonably active, so I have to be careful.

It's a little over an hour before I finally start seeing streetlights on the outskirts of town. My phone dings, and I see it's Garrett. I pull over at a gas station to read it since I'll need to fill up for the drive home anyway.

Hey babe—I'm sorry, but something came up at work. Raincheck?

I stare at the screen. He couldn't have texted me before I left Magnolia Row? He knew I was on the way, and that I was likely close.

I shouldn't be surprised, but I am disappointed—not to mention frustrated. I know he has a lot on his plate with running his own company and all, but still.

Perfectly fine! I'll see you another night. No worries.

I tell myself not to be mad and that it's not about me, but it's hard. This isn't the first time he's done this.

You're the best. Don't know what I'd do without you. We'll try again next week.

I pump gas, then follow the path back to Magnolia Row in the dark. This time I don't listen to any music. I stare blankly at the empty road and passing trees in perfect silence.

I don't want Nana to know what happened, so once I get back to my hometown, I head straight to Cattywampus Brewing. The gravel lot is packed, so I park on Main and walk down to the river.

The brewery is in an old cotton mill. It's a huge, open space with exposed brick and high-top tables dotting the floor. There's a stage opposite the bar, and tonight a country band is playing. They must be from out of town, as I don't recognize any of them.

I spot my friends at a table in the middle of the room.

Sistine waves at me and whispers something to Kendall, which I'm sure is a snide remark about Garrett.

Sistine has wavy blonde hair she keeps shoulder-length and is wearing a loose Magnolia Row High School homecoming shirt from twelve years ago with cut-off jean shorts. She's the opposite of me: short, flat as a fritter in front and back, and doesn't wear a stitch of makeup. Kendall is just as petite, but has a little more of a figure with long, dark hair and minimal, natural make-up. I know it's all in my head, but they both make me feel like a giant clown sometimes.

"Fancy seeing you here," Sistine says as I approach and toss my purse onto the rough wooden table. "What happened to your hot date?"

"He had something come up."

Sistine and Kendall exchange a look. Sistine's says "I told you so," and Kendall's is one of pity.

"What could be more important than seeing you?" asked Sistine.

"He owns that tech company. He's always busy. It's hard right now, but once he gets it up and running with the right managers, we'll spend more time together."

They stare at me like I'm pathetic.

"Stop. Both of you."

"We think you deserve better," says Kendall.

"What I deserve is a drink." I go to the bar and order a Tilted Halo Strawberry Blonde.

"I thought you weren't coming tonight," says Calista, the barkeep who's been here since the place opened several years ago. "Sissy said you had a date."

"Change of plans," I say as she gives me my drink and I hand her my card. As I walk back to the table, Sistine and Kendall stare at me like we have unfinished business.

"So what did he say?" asks Sistine the moment I sit back down.

"Who?" I ask, sipping my beer and playing dumb, as if Garrett cancelling didn't bother me.

Sistine rolls her eyes. "Garrett. Ferret. Whatever his name is. Douchebag in Montgomery."

I take another swig. It's ice cold and feels great in this stuffy room. "Something came up at work. I didn't ask for details."

"Did he at least tell you before you left?" asks Kendall.

"Well, I wasn't at his house yet."

"But you drove all the way to Montgomery." Sistine says it more as a statement than a question.

I sit back with crossed arms and stare at them. "I don't want to talk about this anymore."

"Fine," says Sistine.

We change the subject and talk about our weeks. Sistine owns the coffee shop a few blocks from here and mentions someone from out of town came in a few days ago, claiming to be an architect who is restoring the old hotel.

"Yeah! I met him too!" I say. "He came to the store today to check out the fountain."

"That's amazing!" says Kendall. "I hope they do a good job. My parents said it used to be so beautiful. Too bad it wasn't fixed up for the movie."

A big Hollywood picture recently wrapped filming here. Apparently the director had heard of our town and thought it was the most picturesque place for a movie. Kendall doesn't like to talk about it, but she had a fling with one of the actors.

"They could've cast the architect," says Sistine. "I don't know that I've ever seen a man so striking."

"Well, he'll be back," I say. "He talked to Nana about buying the fountain."

"He wasn't wearing a ring," says Sistine.

"Are you ready to date again?" Kendall asks Sistine, with a hint of hope in her voice. Sistine married her high school sweetheart, as did our friend Patsy, within months of graduating. Patsy went on to have five boys and a happy marriage. Sistine's husband was killed in car accident the day Patsy's first son was born. She and her husband were driving to the hospital to visit the new baby when they were hit, and she still has scars on her scalp and arms from the glass. She hasn't dated since and refuses to talk about it.

"No. I wasn't thinking of me," she says, looking at me and raising her eyebrows.

"I can't go out with him," I say. "I have Garrett. Besides, Rhodes is way out of my league."

"Rhodes?" asks Kendall. "You're on a first-name basis?"

Sistine doesn't miss a beat. "Garrett won't even call you his girlfriend. How long has it been? A year?"

"Sixteen months," I say, sipping my beer again. "It's fine. We're undefinable."

"He's using you to be his secret sex girl." Sistine gives me a look, daring me to challenge her.

"He is not."

"Have you ever met his friends?" she asks, her eyes darting between me and Kendall.

"No."

"Family?"

"No."

"Does he have pictures of you at his house?"

"He lives in an apartment, but no."

"He's a big successful businessman who lives in an apartment?" She gives me a look as if to say 'checkmate.'

"It's a nice-ish apartment."

"Has he ever even come here to see you?"

"No, but with my nana—"

"Whom he's never shown interest in meeting!"

I sigh and slouch my shoulders, glaring at Sistine.

Kendall raises her eyebrows and fidgets with her pint glass. "We can change the subject," she says, shooting Sistine a look imploring her to tone down the interrogation.

"Oh my God," says Sistine, looking towards the bar. "As if the Lord himself heard us. There he is!"

"Who?" I ask, turning around.

Staring right back at me, leaning on the bar and looking oh-so-casually-cool, is Rhodes.

"Who are we looking at?" asks Kendall.

"The hot architect," answers Sistine.

"Oh!" she replies, immediately knowing exactly who we're talking about. "He is hot!"

He waves, and I'm pretty sure he's looking at me. I wave back, feeling all the blood rush to my face, and turn back around.

"Micah, you are blushing!" says Kendall.

"Go get another drink," says Sistine.

"But I still have—"

Sistine picks up my beer and chugs it, then slams the empty glass down on the table.

"Put the next one on my tab. Just get your ass up there."

I roll my eyes but grab my empty glass and make my way to the bar. Rhodes smiles when he sees me approaching.

Micah walks towards me from across the brewery, and I swear time itself comes to a crawl as she moves in slow motion. She's stunning. The dress she's wearing hugs her round hips and is low-cut enough to leave little to the imagination. She doesn't need the sweater she's wearing, which is probably why her face is red since it's so hot, but she's still the most gorgeous person in this room.

"Hi," she says, awkwardly.

"Micah, it's great to see you again." I want to hug her, but that may be weird. And a little forced. I'm so bad at this.

"You aren't stalking me, are you?"

My stomach drops and I feel the blood drain from my face. I mean, I was hoping she'd be here, but I don't think I've reached stalker level.

"No," I say, probably a little more defensively than I meant. "Not at all. I didn't know—"

"I was joking," she says, grabbing my arm. "Bad joke. I'm sorry."

I sigh in relief and feel a tingle of electricity run to my spine from her hand touching my skin. "No, it's fine. I'm going back tomorrow. I just wanted to check out the town a bit."

"What do you think so far?" she asks as she gets the bartender's attention and hands off her empty glass.

"You know, I'd heard about Magnolia Row, but I had no idea it would be so eclectic. It's a nice surprise. Everything has so much personality, down to the wood grain. It's refreshing."

"Well, don't go telling everyone about us. We like to keep this place a secret."

I smile and take a sip of my beer. "Did you grow up here?" I ask, desperate to keep the conversation going.

"Yep," she says, taking a fresh drink from the blonde lady behind the bar, who winks at her then looks at me.

"Put it on my tab," I tell her.

"Thank you," Micah says, lowering her head shyly. "I live with my nana. She has some health issues and can't live alone or drive, so I take care of her."

"That's sweet. You two seem close."

"Yeah, she's my best friend. She's raised me since I was little."

I don't pry, but I can tell Micah probably had a rough childhood. Kids raised by grandparents aren't with their parents for a reason.

"What about you? Have you always lived in Birmingham?"

"Basically, yeah. I grew up in the suburbs, then went to Auburn for architecture school. I moved back after graduation and have been there since."

"You must like living there," she says, fidgeting with her hair like she's nervous.

"I can't complain."

She looks back towards her table, where her friends are staring at us.

"Is that the girl from the coffee shop?" I ask.

"Yeah, Sistine. She owns it. She mentioned she met you."

I laugh. "Word travels fast."

"Welcome to Magnolia Row! Any time a stranger blows through, the whole town knows about it. A big movie finished filming here a few months ago, so you can imagine the excitement that brought."

"Absolutely. It's the perfect place for filming. It's like going back in time. If I were a director, I'd absolutely want to shoot something here."

There was an awkward pause as we nursed our beers and stared awkwardly at one another.

"I don't want to keep you from your friends," I say. "But if you're free tomorrow, I'd love to take you to lunch before I hit the road."

"She'd love to," a voice says from behind me. I turn around to see a petite brunette with a big smile on her face.

"This is my friend, Kendall," Micah says, and I reach out my hand.

"Rhodes Cauley."

She stares at us, smiling.

"Um, yeah, I guess we can do lunch," says Micah, giving Kendall the stink eye.

"Great! What's good?"

"We can meet at Bread Crumbs at eleven?"

"Oh, yeah! It's right by the coffee shop on Main Street. I saw it when I got to town."

"That's it!"

"Awesome! Well, I'll leave you ladies alone. See you tomorrow, Micah."

"Sounds good."

Kendall grabs Micah's arm and leads her back to the table. I watch as they sit and the faces of Sistine and Kendall light up, though Micah's back is to me.

I turn to the bar, run my hands through my hair, and sigh. My first date since my divorce. It's been five years, so it's definitely time to put myself out there. I hope I don't come across as uncomfortable as I feel.

I stay and pretend to listen to the band for a bit, nursing my beer and catching Micah's eye on more than one occasion. She and her friends are obviously talking about me like schoolgirls at the lunch table, but it's cute. It makes me feel young again.

I finish my drink, pay, and on my way out the door, I glance back to see Micah staring in my direction. She grins, embarrassed I caught her looking, and turns around to her friends. I grin, leaving the brewery with a light nervousness that makes me feel thirty years younger.

MICAH

"*M*icah has a daaaaaate!" Kendall tells Sistine when we sit back down.

Sistine squeals and claps her hands. It's rare to see her happy since her husband died, so even if tomorrow goes poorly, at least I was able to give her this moment.

"Y'all need to stop," I say.

"Where are y'all going?" asks Sistine.

"Bread Crumbs," I answer. "Tomorrow. It's not a big deal."

"Wear something super low-cut," says Kendall.

"Most of Micah's clothes are low-cut, if you haven't noticed," says Sistine, eying my cleavage.

"If you got it, flaunt it!" Kendall says. "I'm jealous."

"I don't need this, y'all. I have Garrett. It doesn't feel right."

"If Garrett gave a damn about you," says Sistine, "you'd be with him tonight. As it is, you're here. And so is Mr. Sexy Architect Man."

I look over at Rhodes, who is leaning against the bar and enjoying the band. He catches me look at him and gives a polite, shy smile. I look away quickly.

"That guy is way too hot for me."

"Whatever!" says Sistine. "You're gorgeous, you have curves for days, and you're extremely smart, which I'm sure Mr. Sexy Architect Man will love."

"Please stop calling him that."

Kendall and Sistine both giggle and eye one another.

I know my friends like to pump me up, and they may actually see me in a flattering light, but it's hard to feel it myself. I've always been the chubby girl. Even when we were little, I was the fat friend. They had guys chasing after them; I never did. Before I moved in with Nana, my mom put me on every fad diet she came across and even bought me clothes that were too small to try to motivate me to lose weight. I only got bigger. Luckily, as I got taller, the weight seemed to distribute itself better around my body, but I'm still not thin. My boobs hurt my back, I have birthing hips, and my bubble butt makes it hard to find jeans that fit properly. And I'm broad. My shoulders are the size of Kendall's and Sistine's combined.

"Besides," says Kendall, "if *he* thought he was too hot for you, he wouldn't have asked you out."

"Is he too old?" I ask. "He looks older."

"It's not like he's on Medicare," says Sistine, rolling her eyes. "Stop looking for excuses. Go out with him. Give him a chance."

"Fine," I say.

The rest of the night we listen to the band, have a few

more drinks, and I catch Rhodes' eye before he quietly slips out. Not once throughout the night did I see him checking out my friends, or any other girl for that matter. It's strange.

When I get home, Nana is asleep on the couch. I wake her, make sure she takes her last round of meds for the day, and help her to bed. She asks me if I had fun, and I simply tell her yes without letting her know I'd been stood up.

The less she knows, the less she worries.

I return to my room, put on my pajamas, and collapse on my four-poster bed. My room is still pink from when I was little, though I removed my holiday Barbies and Beanie Babies from the bookshelf quite a few years ago. They were replaced with romance novels, candles, and photos from high school. The bedrooms in the house have white shag carpet, which is in remarkable condition given how old it is.

I turn on some music from my phone and lay for a while, listening to Taylor Swift and thinking about Garrett and my date with Rhodes tomorrow. I like to pretend it doesn't bother me when Garrett flakes, but the truth is it hurts like hell. And it happens a lot, more than even my friends know. I make excuses for him all the time, but it gets to a point where I simply want to know he cares about me. I like to think I'm above it, that it doesn't affect me, but I guess I'm lying to myself. Someone who cares about you wouldn't let you drive over an hour to see them, only to cancel at the last minute. I know he's busy with work, but he shouldn't have let me travel all that way before changing his mind.

I sigh, then roll out of bed to wash off my makeup and brush my teeth. I'm not even sure how I feel about this date with Rhodes. I reckon I'll show up and see how it goes. Then I'll decide what I want from him, if anything.

I'm so tired of thinking about men. They're never worth it.

RHODES

I check out of the hotel and arrive at Bread Crumbs early. They're still serving breakfast, and it smells like bacon and eggs. My stomach howls, but I sate it with a simple bottle of water while I wait for Micah.

I'm scrolling through pictures my son posted from a law school party when Micah walks in at exactly eleven o'clock. The whole energy of the place shifts, like a fresh spring breeze wafting through the door. She's wearing red lipstick, dark jeans, an open knit sweater over a tank top, and sandals with flowers on them. Her bright red hair is down, and the waves frame her face perfectly. She's a vision.

I stand up to meet her and we hug before sitting down. The waitress comes over and hands us paper menus, but Micah puts hers down without looking at it.

"I always get the fried green tomato BLT," she tells me. "It has an amazing aioli sauce."

"Sounds delicious," I say, putting my menu down. "Thank you for meeting me for lunch."

"Thank you for asking me," she says. "It's not every day a handsome stranger shows up in town and asks me out, so this is new."

My heart flutters when she calls me handsome, and I'm surprised by how forward she is. "I don't know about being handsome, but I'm delighted to be here with you."

"Oh, please," said Micah. "Every girl at Cattywampus was staring at you last night."

I shake my head. "They were probably wondering who the weirdo alone at the bar was."

"Nope. Trust me."

"Do you go to Cattywampus often?" I ask, then take a sip of my water.

"Most weekends. That's pretty much where everyone goes to hang out, whether they drink or not."

"It's a cool space. It used to be a mill?"

"Cotton mill. You'll find that most of the buildings around town are old and repurposed in some way."

"I love it. That's what I do. I recently started my own firm specializing in historic restoration work."

Her face lit up. "Wow! A man after my own heart. I love old things."

The first thought that crossed my mind was maybe, as an old thing myself, she could love me too. I'm tempted to ask about her age, but I don't want to come off as rude. From a distance, she looks like she's in her twenties, but on closer examination, she has a few fine lines around her mouth and eyes, so I'm hoping she's at least thirty.

"Me too," I say. "I love the history and personality in these buildings. Each one has a story, like the table in your shop. The wood and tile speak to you when you walk in. It's a spiritual experience, really, to exist in a space with so many stories."

She smiles.

"Is that weird?" I ask.

"Not at all."

The waitress comes and we order our BLTs.

"So," says Micah after she leaves, "tell me about yourself."

"Well," I begin. This feels like a job interview. "I live in Birmingham, as you know. I have one son, who is twenty-three. He recently started law school at Alabama, which is crazy to think about. I can't believe I have a son old enough for grad school."

She raises her eyebrows and makes a surprised face. "Wow. That's impressive."

"What? My son being in law school or me being old enough to have a son in law school?"

"Both. You don't look old enough to have a grown kid."

"I'm forty-five. He was born while I was in college, which was tough, but my former wife was a rockstar mom. She took care of him and worked so I could finish school." There's a pause in conversation, and I decide to bite the bullet and ask the one thing I know you aren't supposed to mention on an early date. "How old are you?" I say. I have to know, to make sure I'm not a creep going after a girl my son's age.

"Thirty," she says, making a face like she can't believe she's admitting to it.

"Thirty is young," I say in an attempt to reassure her, but in reality I think I'm trying to wrap my head around it. She's closer to my son's age than mine. I was learning to drive when she was learning to walk. That's a little weird to think about, but I push it to the back of my mind. At least she's not in her twenties. That would be too weird.

"So you're divorced?" she asks.

"Yes. Five years now. Right after Mason went to college, we separated. She had met someone else and waited until Mason was grown to pursue it."

"Wow," she says, her eyes dropping. "I'm sorry."

I shrug my shoulders. "To be fair, I was a little too career-obsessed and wasn't home much when she was doing all the work to raise our son. That's my one regret in life. But it is what it is, and I think we're all happier now, including Mason."

"That's good," she says. "So your son handled it well?"

"He was shocked at first, especially since it wasn't a situation where Mom and Dad were fighting all the time. We never talked at all, so he didn't see it coming. He's okay now. He stays with his mom and her new partner at their lake house a lot. I think he's accepted this as the new normal."

"Yeah, that's a lot to wrap your head around."

"It is, but he's a great kid. Well, I call him a kid. He's grown, which still blows my mind." I drink my water and clear my throat. "What about you? Any kids?"

"No, my nana is enough of a handful," she laughs. "I can't handle anyone else."

"Sounds like it." I almost ask her if she wants kids, but I know that's not first-date conversation. I will need to know at some point, assuming we make it past this lunch date. If she has dreams of a young husband and a house full of babies, I'm not the guy for her, despite how gorgeous and captivating she is. I can't go back to diapers and t-ball.

I decide to change the subject. "What was it like to grow up here? In a town this magical, it had to be like something out of a Hallmark movie."

"Well, I thought it was boring when I was younger, and I guess it was, especially for a high schooler. There wasn't much to do besides wander the cemeteries and break into old houses."

"Seriously?" I ask with a small chuckle.

"Oh, yeah. There's an old graveyard on the other side of the historic district where we used to walk at night, and if you drive about a mile past the Florablanca Inn, there's a dilapidated house on the river in the Victorian Village where we would go to drink and hang out."

"Okay, now that sounds like a horror movie."

"No, it's absolutely enchanting. I love that house. I wish I could afford to buy it and fix it up. I guess that's my dream in life. If I win the lottery, that's what I'm doing."

"That's a good dream," I say. "I'd love to see it sometime."

She nods, fingering her glass of water. She seems anxious somehow and it's flattering, not to mention adorable.

"So the Victorian Village…I heard most of the houses are gone?"

"Yeah, unfortunately. Only a few are left. A massive lightning fire took out a lot of what was on that street before I was born."

"It was one street full of Victorian houses?"

"Yep! There are photos at the Finnegan House. The Florablanca Inn was the star of the street, though. I'm so glad it's still there."

"I went to Finnegan House. They gave me an album of hotel photos."

"Nice!" An awkward silence settles over us for a few moments, and I take the opportunity to notice how nervous she is. It's endearing.

"So," she finally asks, "you went to Auburn? Kendall went there too."

"Yeah, I loved it. It's a great town. Did you go to college?"

"Just one semester at Savannah College of Art and Design."

"Wow! I love Savannah. The GC I'm wanting to use for the hotel is out of Savannah."

"GC?"

"General contractor."

"Ah," she says with a nod. "Yes, I absolutely adored Savannah. I could've stayed there forever if things had been different."

"What happened?"

"Nana was already starting to go downhill when I left, but during my first semester she had a heart attack while she was driving. She veered off the road and hit a tree. She's lucky she even survived. When I came home, I realized her blood sugar was out of control. She really wasn't taking care of herself, so I decided to quit college and stay."

"That's a very selfless thing to do."

"Quite the opposite. Sometimes I think I'm forcing her to live for me. She dropped everything to take care of me when she didn't have to, so I'm returning the favor."

I smile and resist the urge to take her hand. I want to, but it feels like too much.

Our food comes, and it smells amazing.

"This is the best sandwich you'll ever put in your mouth," says Micah. She takes a bite and somehow manages to not mess up her bright red lipstick.

I try it and my taste buds are immediately overwhelmed. The spice from the aioli, the salt from the bacon, the bitter of the green tomato, and the sweet bread meld together into an explosion of Southern fried goodness on my tongue.

"I may never go back to Birmingham," I say after swallowing. "You weren't kidding. This is wonderful!"

She laughs. "Told you! I love this place."

We each take another bite, and it's all I can do not to roll my eyes back in my head. I grew up on Southern food, yet this is the most delicious fried green tomato I've ever had in my life.

"What do you do in Birmingham?" she asks after downing a gulp of water.

"Work, mostly. I know that's boring, but it's true."

"What kind of projects do you normally do?"

"Well, at my old job we were doing a lot of commercial buildings, office spaces, things like that. It was good money, but I wasn't passionate about it. I started moonlighting to help a firm out of Nashville on some historic restorations and fell in love with architecture all over again. After my divorce, I figured it was now or never, so I opened my own firm. I've worked on a few houses in north Alabama, but the Florablanca Inn is my biggest and most challenging job. The lady who owns it is kinda crazy, but I'm pretty ecstatic about the project overall. It'll probably consume the next year of my life, but there's nothing else I'd rather be doing."

"That's incredible. It's good to know your passion."

I nod. "What were you planning to study at SCAD?"

"Preservation design."

"A woman after my own heart! You would've been great. I can tell by the way your store is laid out that you have a great eye."

"Thank you. I recently helped redecorate my friend Kendall's house. She's divorced, so our friend Patsy and I completely changed her entire house to erase all traces of her ex-husband. It was SO much fun. We basically took everything out and started with a blank slate."

"I'd love to see it."

She pulls out her phone and scrolls through the pictures. I continue eating my sandwich as she shows me shot after shot of this beautiful house full of light on the river. She narrates each room, showing me what they added and describing how it looked before. It had an eclectic mix of antiques and new furniture and was decorated with massive photo prints of local sites and white architectural pieces. It's feminine and classy, like Micah. Her face lights up and her green eyes sparkle when she talks about it.

"Did any of that come from your store?" I ask.

"Oh, yes! A lot of it did."

I'd love to set her loose in my loft. When I moved in, I thought it would be fun to decorate in earthy grays and dark colors with crisp, clean lines, but now it feels too masculine and cold, like I live in a factory. A woman's touch would do it some good.

We continue to chat about our favorite books and movies while we finish our sandwiches. I tell her about my wealthy, eccentric client and her plans for the hotel. After about two hours, we wrap up the date and I walk her to her car.

"What are you up to the rest of the day?" I ask.

"I left Nana alone at the store, so I need to make sure she took her meds. Once we close up, I'll probably go home and read."

"Well, I'll definitely be stopping by the store in the next few weeks. Don't let the fountain get away from me."

"It's been there for as long as I can remember. It's not going anywhere, I promise."

Her hair is so bright it looks like it could burst into flame in this hot sun. I want to run my hands through it, but even I know that would be weird. In fact, I'm not sure how to close this date.

"Thank you, Micah, for meeting me today. I really enjoy talking to you."

"Me too. I mean, you know, I enjoy talking to you. Not myself." She shakes her head and closes her eyes. "I'm sorry. I'm so bad at this. It's no wonder I'm still single."

I laugh. "No, you're great. I'm just as bad, if not worse, I promise."

I give her a hug, and she hugs me back. Her body is warm against mine and even though it's a hundred degrees outside with high humidity, I want to hold her here forever.

"See you soon," I say. She waves goodbye and gets in her car. I watch as she backs out and drives down Main Street.

It's only after she disappears that I realize I'd failed to get her number.

MICAH

"Hey, Nana!" I call as I enter the store. It's hotter in here than it is outside. If Hell was an antique store, this would be it.

"I'm in here!" she calls from the office. I can barely hear her above the box fan she has directed at her face. Every paper on her desk is weighed down to keep it from blowing away.

"We have to get a new air conditioner," I say. "I can't live like this anymore." I go behind the desk and take out a rubber band to pull my hair back.

"Are you going to tell me who you went to lunch with?" she asks.

"A friend."

She eyes me and cocks and eyebrow. "A girl friend?"

I sigh. "No."

She leans back in her chair, takes off her reading glasses, and taps them on her mouth. "Don't tell me that boy in Montgomery finally decided to put forth a little effort and come see you for a change."

"No."

"I didn't think so." She places her glasses on the desk, waiting for me to elaborate.

I stare back at her. She's not going to let this go.

"You know the architect who came in yesterday?" Her face lights up like a Christmas tree. "I had lunch with him."

"Oh, Micah! I'm so excited for you! He looks like he stepped right out of a magazine."

"I am aware." I try to be as curt as possible and not let her know I basically floated to work on a cloud.

"When did he ask you out? I didn't hear him ask when he was in the store."

"You were in the office half the time."

"Honey, you know I was eavesdropping."

I sigh and give her a look. "I saw him at Cattywampus last night. He asked me then."

"I thought you were in Montgomery last night."

"That didn't work out."

"Of course it didn't."

"Nana," I say, warning her I don't want to talk about it.

"So you broke up with Garrett and now you're with Rhodes?" she asks. I don't like how my life sounds like a soap opera coming out of her mouth.

"No, it was one lunch. That's it. No big deal."

"When are you going out again?"

"I don't know. He didn't ask me. He didn't kiss me. He didn't get my phone number. It was probably a waste of time." I cross my arms and cock my head to one side.

"Don't say that, sugar. You never know. Some men don't know how to navigate these things."

"He's way too good for me."

"Oh, hush up. No one is too good for you."

"He is. You saw him. He's tall and lean and handsome. I'm a fat frumpy mess."

"You are not. If you keep talking like that, I'll put salt in your tea."

I roll my eyes. "He did say he wants the fountain. Are you willing to part with it?"

"If I get a good price for it, I will. It would be nice to see it back in the hotel."

"From what he says, the owner has deep pockets and is a little nuts."

"Nothing wrong with that, sugar. We're all a little crazy."

I check Nana's pill case and it looks like she did take her meds. I take a sip of her tea and confirm yes, she did use artificial sweetener for once. She shakes her head at me. I know she hates me treating her like a child, but I can't trust her to take care of herself.

"Oh!" she says, putting her glasses back on and flipping open her calendar. "I got a call from Julian George. You know that big farmhouse on the highway between here and Monroeville? It's set way back off the road and has the white fence that's falling down."

"Yes, vaguely."

"The owners finally died, and Julian's handling the sale of the house for their kids. They're having a huge estate sale in a few weeks and he's giving us first dibs."

"Awesome! How soon can we go?"

"He said the kids want to come get pictures and senti-mental stuff first, but he's going to let me know."

This is refreshing. The store has been looking a little empty since we decorated Kendall's house. Maybe we'll have some new stuff to show Rhodes next time he comes.

I check myself. This is bad. This is very, very bad. I don't need to be thinking about Rhodes. I have Garrett.

I look at my phone and suddenly realize I haven't heard from—nor thought about hearing from—Garrett today until this very moment.

Huh. That's a change.

I go out to the floor with my duster, straighten up a few things, and help a customer looking for a lamp. Once the day is done, I take Nana home as usual and hide in my room, trying not to think about Rhodes.

Of course, the group text I have with Kendall, Patsy, and Sistine starts blowing up. Sistine and Kendall fill Patsy in on my "big date," then they pester me until I finally respond that I don't want to talk about it. Patsy vows not to miss the next girls' night, though I know this is a tall order since she has five small boys at home.

Nana and I bake chicken and asparagus and eat dinner while watching Hallmark movies. She doesn't say anything else about Rhodes, thankfully.

After we eat, I make sure she takes her meds before I return to my room, where I put on some music (Kacey Musgraves, of course), and make the mistake of going down an online rabbit hole to stalk Rhodes.

I find the website for his architecture firm, which

includes an oh-so-sexy photo of him in front of a Victorian home. His arms are crossed and his body somehow looks even taller than in person. The blue tie he's wearing makes his eyes pop, and he has a serious but approachable expression on his face.

I can't believe this guy ever asked me out. He's big-city, hyper-educated, smoldering-sexy professional man. I'm small-town, live-with-my-nana, awkward chubby girl. No wonder he didn't ask for my number.

I move to social media. I find his professional sites, which have a few photos of historic homes he's worked on. His personal profiles are scant at best, though I did find his ex-wife in an old photo with a link to her profile. While it was set to private, I could see a profile picture of her with their son. He looks young in the picture, but I can definitely see the resemblance between him and Rhodes. He has the same dark hair and bright eyes, though the shape of his face is more like his mom's. The ex-wife is beautiful, of course. She's short and toned, like she spends a lot of time at the gym.

I do not.

This leaves me even more confused. I look nothing like this woman. Maybe he doesn't have a type?

I need to stop obsessing. It's becoming unhealthy.

A week goes by, and of course I don't hear anything from Rhodes, though Garrett texts a few times to let me know he's thinking about me.

On Saturday night, I meet up with Sistine, Kendall, and Patsy for drinks at Cattywampus.

"I have one hour," says Patsy when she sits down, her bleach-blonde hair bouncing over her bare shoulders. "Garion is helping his brother dig a pit to roast a hog and Mama can only watch the kids until seven. So, Micah, spit it out. What happened with Mr. Sexy Architect Man?"

I roll my eyes and look at the other two, who give me doe eyes as they drink their beer. I go through the whole spiel about how we met, running into him here at the brewery, and lunch the next day.

"He sounds like a dream!" says Patsy.

"You should see him," says Sistine.

"Is he hotter than Kendall's movie star man?"

Kendall rolls her eyes.

"Comparable," answers Sistine. "Seriously. He's gorgeous."

"Well, he's gotta be better than Garrett the Douchebag. I heard he stood you up the other night after you'd already driven all the way to Montgomery."

Again, I give Sistine and Kendall the stink eye. "He was busy."

"Oh he's always f-ing busy. Busy thinking he can string you along while he does whatever and whomever he wants up there, while you sit around waiting for him down here."

"I'm done talking about Garrett."

"Just be done with Garrett," says Sistine. "Then we won't have to talk about him."

"Y'all are making me feel like crap right now," I say. "Besides, Garrett has actually texted me this week. Rhodes has not. He didn't even get my number. Didn't kiss me. Nothing. I know he wants the fountain from the store, so I assume I'll see him again, but I'm pretty sure it ends there."

Kendall holds my hand across the table. "We didn't mean to make you feel like crap," she says.

Patsy touches my back. "Yeah, sweetie. We want you to be happy, and Garrett does not make you happy."

"Even if things don't work out with Rhodes," says Sistine, "we want you to know you deserve a guy in that league. You're beautiful, and—"

"Y'all, please stop. I'm done with this conversation. Let me live my life."

We all get quiet and finish our beer. The rest of the night, we gossip about Kendall's ex-husband, the drunk girl at the bar, and Patsy's brother's baby mama drama.

At the end of the night, I go home, check on Nana, and listen to music while I fall asleep. I try thinking about Garrett, but find my mind wandering to Rhodes time and time again.

RHODES

eeks have gone by since I left Magnolia Row. I've buried myself in work on the Florablanca Inn project and barely left my condo, which now seems cold and unfeeling after being in the warm, cozy, small town environment.

Nevertheless, I've trapped myself in here to finish this proposal. I'm surprised my neighbors haven't called for a wellness check. I pace the cold hardwood floor, eat frozen dinners, and work. Sometimes I sleep, but even then, I dream about work.

My friend Jaxon agrees to handle general contractor duties for the hotel, which is fantastic since he exclusively works on historic buildings and is the only person I trust with an undertaking this large. He's working on getting a structural engineer, an electrician to replace the knob-and-tube electrical system, and some local guys for the plaster and plumbing work.

Once I finish my final proposal, complete with estimates, blueprints, sketches, and an overall description of my vision for the project, I call my client.

"Wilhelmina," she says, answering the phone as if introducing herself.

"Um, hi, Mrs. Caxton?"

"It's Wilhelmina, darling. Don't be so formal."

"Oh, um, I'm sorry. I thought you said—"

"Yes, well, I changed my mind." Her voice echoes like I'm on speakerphone. I imagine her with a glass of red wine and doing her makeup in one of those mirrors with the big lightbulbs all around it.

"Okay, uh, Wilhelmina. This is Rhodes Cauley, the architect you—"

"Yes, Rhodes. I know who you are. I had my assistant program my phone so that your picture pops up when you call. How are things coming along?"

I ignore the picture comment. "I have the final proposal ready to send you. The only thing missing is the price of the fountain. I located the original to the lobby of the hotel, but I'm not sure how much they want for it."

"However much it's worth, double it if we have to. Everything has a price, darling."

"Um, okay." I'm not sure how to respond. Her flippant approach to finances makes me a little uncomfortable, so I move on. "I included the fountain in my design, assuming we can get it. Do you want me to email this all to you, or do you want to meet in Magnolia Row sometime soon?"

"How is next week? Maybe Thursday? We can meet on site. I hate computers. Never email me anything. I won't see it. Besides, I haven't been around a good-looking man all month and I'd love to see you."

I shake my head. "Yes, ma'am. Thursday works fine. How's one o'clock?"

"Don't call me ma'am. It's Wilhelmina. And one o'clock is perfect."

We hang up. I sit on my black leather sofa, look past the bustling city towards Red Mountain, and sigh.

Going back to Magnolia Row will mean seeing Micah again, finally. For the past few weeks, I've been kicking myself for not getting her number or at least going in for a kiss. She probably thinks I forgot about her. I really blew the ending of that date.

Maybe I should've tried harder to call her before now. Bonaventure Antiques has a website with a number listed, but I'm scared her grandmother will answer and it'll be awkward. I found Micah on social media and thought of adding her as a friend, but I'm not sure if that's creepy. I wish there were some kind of guide to modern dating that outlined exactly what to say and what to do on which dates. At first, I felt like I shouldn't call because it was too soon, but now I feel like it's been too long. This game is impossible to navigate.

I lean back on the couch and run my fingers through my hair. I'm way too old for this. Restoring a huge hotel that's been neglected for thirty years is easier than trying to figure out when and whether I should call someone I'm interested in. It shouldn't be this complicated. I like her. I should call.

There is one thing, though — Micah's age. Fifteen years

is a big difference. What if she wants kids? With a son in college, I don't want to go back to being a dad to a little one. I'm looking forward to grandkids down the road, but that's it.

I know I'm getting way ahead of myself. I need to focus on work and stop obsessing like a teenager.

I send a text to Jaxon and he agrees to meet me in Magnolia Row next Thursday. He and I will meet that morning, go to lunch, then see Wilhelmina in the afternoon. Hopefully I can sneak in an hour or so to go to Micah's store and get a few pictures of the fountain, maybe talk to her grandmother about a price, and secure at least one more date if I haven't already blown it.

In the meantime, I can't get her out of my head. I can tell by the way she talks about things, the aesthetic of the store, and her style that she and I are cut from the same cloth. We both love old things—love their energy, their life. I've never met another woman quite like her. I could talk to her all day and stare at her all night.

Now I'm feeling creepy again.

I still can't get a handle on having a crush. It's scary and invigorating.

On top of that, I'm enraptured by the town of Magnolia Row. I love everything about it, and Micah is a living, breathing embodiment of everything the place has to offer. Coming back to my cold loft in the steel city was hard. I used to love where I live, but now I'm feeling homesick for a place—and a person—I've only spent a few days with.

I can't wait to go back.

MICAH

It's early Thursday morning, and though the weather is cooler thanks to the overnight rain, it left a thick, suffocating veil of humidity in the air.

Nana and I are busy taking inventory of how much space we have for new things. And by new, I mean new to us. We're going to the estate sale tomorrow, to which Julian is giving us early access. He sent us photos of the house already, and to say it's a goldmine would be an understatement. I'm not sure what these people did or how long they lived there, but they must have had deep pockets. There are so many items I want, most of them large and bulky. I told Nana I'm not above getting a storage unit if we fill up the rectory so we can get as much as we want.

I call Patsy's husband, Garion, who runs a construction business. He assures me he and one of his crew will be able to meet us with a large moving truck late tomorrow afternoon if we need them to, which is good, since Nana and I obviously can't move heavy furniture by ourselves.

I'm on my hands and knees on the floor, booty facing the front door of course, trying to find the plug for a lamp when the bell jingles, signaling someone has walked into the store.

I turn around and it's Rhodes. Of course it is. I'm looking at him from around my big old booty when he smiles and waves.

I am humiliated. Blood rushes to my cheeks and I want to sink into the floor and melt like the witch in *The Wizard of Oz*.

"Rhodes!" says Nana, exiting her office.

I stand, biting my lip and shaking my head. This was not the impression I wanted to make when I saw him again.

"Hello, Ms. Bonaventure."

"Please, honey. Call me Barbara."

He smiles. "Barbara." He turns to me. "Micah, it's wonderful to see you again."

I nod, trying to forget he saw my rear-end in the air moments before. "You too, Rhodes."

He turns to Nana. "Have you decided to sell the fountain? Just so you know, my client will pay whatever you ask, whether it's working or not."

"She'll have to if she wants it," says Nana, who returns to her office to get the paperwork for the fountain.

He returns his attention to me. "You look very nice today," he says, and for a moment it seems like he's blushing.

"Thank you," I say before Nana comes back in the room.

She hands a folder to Rhodes. He opens it, raises his eyebrows, and says, "I think that's fair for something this unique. Do you mind if I take some photos? I'm meeting with her this afternoon and would love to show her."

"Absolutely," Nana says. I back away from the fountain and stand in the office door with Nana to avoid being in the pictures.

"We can get afford a new air conditioner now," she whispers, jabbing me in the side with her elbow.

"Thank you, Jesus," I murmur back.

"How did you get it in here?" Rhodes asks as he's snapping away.

"Very carefully," answers Nana. "We had to take the doors off the hinges, and it took six grown men to finagle it."

"So it should be fun getting it out?" he asks, grinning.

"I'll leave that up to you," she says. "I certainly can't move it."

Once he has about thirty photos, he walks over and offers his hand to Nana.

"Honey, we hug in this store," she says, grabbing him and wrapping her arms around him. She holds him for longer than she should and peers around his arm to wink at me.

I roll my eyes.

"Of course," he says. He turns his attention to me. "Micah, I have a business associate in town today, but I'd love to take you to lunch tomorrow before I go back to Birmingham."

"Oh, I can't," I say. I feel myself blush again. I hate that I turn bright red every time he looks at me. I don't even need a mirror to see it—the heat is radiating from my face. It's so embarrassing. "We're closing the shop tomorrow to go to an estate sale outside of town."

"Oh, that's too bad," he says with a look of disappointment that makes me feel awful. He pulls out his phone, but Nana interrupts him.

"Why don't you come with us?" she asks. "There's plenty of room in the car."

I open my mouth to object, then realize I have no idea why I'm objecting. I've been obsessing over this man for weeks now. Maybe it's the weirdness of hanging out with him and my grandmother together all day? I should be jumping at the chance to see him, but it does feel a little awkward.

"I'd love to go," says Rhodes before I can think of anything to say.

"Wonderful! We can pick you up. Where are you staying?"

"The Mossy River Motel south of town."

"Great!" says Nana. "That's on our way."

Rhodes looks at me, and I simply smile.

"We'll pick you up at eight."

"Perfect! If you'll excuse me, I have a meeting with my GC at the Florablanca Inn. I'll see both of you tomorrow."

"We're looking forward to it," says Nana.

He nods at her, then puts his hand on my arm. I feel my entire body turn to mush, and not from the heat. "Goodbye, Micah."

"Bye," I say, my voice sounding weak and squeaky. He makes me nervous, like he's so dreamy it wipes my brain.

"Well," says Nana after he walks out, "we may need an extra storage unit after all. We'll have a lot of room after the fountain is removed, but who knows how long that'll take."

"I'll talk to Garion."

The rest of the day we spend compacting as much as we can without compromising the navigability and aesthetic of the store. It keeps me busy, which is good, since it also prevents me from obsessing about Rhodes and wondering what I'm going to wear tomorrow.

We go home late, and I'm in the middle of baking salmon and green beans for our dinner when I get a text from Garrett.

Hey sexy – wanna come over tomorrow night?

I pause.

Normally I'd drop everything and jump at the chance to see him. He has so little free time, and this is the first instance he's wanted to see me since the weekend he cancelled at the last minute.

But I hesitate.

First off, it'll be a busy day as it is. The house we're going to is 45 minutes in the opposite direction, and I have no idea what time we'll get back.

But the biggest factor is Rhodes. I'm spending all day with him. What if he wants to do dinner? Should I keep my schedule open? Or is it sad and pathetic of me to hope for that?

And who am I, juggling two guys? This is not my style at all. I feel like I've entered an alternate universe.

I put my phone down without responding when the oven timer goes off. I take the food out, plate it, and walk to the living room. I place Nana's dinner on her TV tray and curl up on the couch to watch reruns of *Golden Girls*. I leave my phone in the kitchen, but it dings again, so I get up to check it. It's Garrett again.

I miss you.

Just like that, my decision is made.

I'd love to see you tomorrow night. I miss you too.

This is a first. He's never said that before. It's the closest thing to *I love you* he's ever said. Hell, it's the closest thing to *I love you* any guy has ever said to me.

I pocket my phone and go back to the sofa and pretend to pay attention to the television while I think about the next day.

Now I have to plan two sexy outfits.

My day in Magnolia Row is hyper-productive. I meet with Jaxon and we do an in-depth inspection of the hotel. He has a structural engineer lined up to come to the property next week. We have lunch, catch up, and present our plans to Wilhelmina. She flirts so hard with Jaxon I think she's going to take her clothes off right there in the ruins of the old hotel lobby, but I'm glad her attention is off me for the moment.

By far, the highlight of the day is seeing Micah. I could tell she was awkward, and I don't blame her. I guess I was sending some mixed signals with the whole go-on-a-date-without-following-up thing, but hopefully I'll make up for it on my outing with her and her grandmother, which I admit is an odd second date. Or maybe it's not a date? I don't even know anymore.

After a night of restless sleep, I'm sitting in the cheap hotel chair in my room, looking out the window, waiting for them to pick me up. I extended my stay by one day in the hopes of having dinner with Micah tonight, so I haven't checked out yet.

My button-down and khakis with dress shoes are probably too dressy for today, but those are the clothes I brought, so they'll have to do. Micah's blue hatchback pulls into the parking lot, so I put my keys, wallet, and phone in my pockets and meet them outside.

It's only eight in the morning—the sun is still low in the sky—and it's already blazing hot. I should've brought lighter clothes to wear.

I get into the back seat of the car on the passenger side, mostly so I can see Micah better.

"Good morning, Rhodes," says Ms. Barbara.

"Good morning, ladies."

Micah smiles at me. Her thick hair is down and she has it wrapped over one shoulder. She's wearing a long white linen dress with a lavender cardigan. The dress is cut low, showing off an amethyst necklace with matching earrings.

"So where is this place?" I ask.

"About forty-five minutes from here," answers Micah. "It's a beautiful house. I can't wait to see the inside."

"I assume the owners passed away?"

"Yes," answered Ms. Barbara. "The real estate agent is meeting us there. He does appraisals for these estate sales in addition to selling houses."

"That's convenient," I say.

On the drive, Micah is mostly quiet while Ms. Barbara points out various landmarks and tells me the history of the area. She's lived in this part of Alabama her entire life, so it seems like she has a story for every mailbox we pass.

She speaks with a deep, musical drawl that is rare nowadays, even in the South. It's a generational accent slowly being lost. I could listen to her all day.

Finally, Micah pulls off the highway and turns down a long driveway with old white fencing on each side. It looks like there used to be cows or horses on the massive property, but the land has been left fallow for what looks like years.

The house itself is stunning. It's a late Victorian farmhouse—dating from the 1890s, I would guess—and though it's clearly been neglected for some time, it has a lot of character. It doesn't have the dainty, gingerbread house-looking woodwork a lot of people associate with Victorian architecture, but it has the characteristic gabled roof and bay windows with a huge wraparound porch.

We get out of the car and approach the house. There's another car in the driveway, which I presume belongs to the realtor/estate sale manager. The haint blue paint on the ceiling of the porch is flaking off, and the boards below our feet creak.

"Hello!" says the realtor with a huge grin as he opens the door. His dark skin sets off his chalky-white hair, and his bright blue suit is complete with a tie.

"Julian, you must be hot as blazes in that coat," Ms. Barbara says when we approach.

"Oh, I got the air cranking, baby. It'll be cool in here in no time."

We enter the foyer, which is packed with massive ornate furniture, huge vases, a grandfather clock that is remarkably operable despite its obvious age, and a two-inch-thick rug spanning nearly the entire length of the house. I glance into some of the adjoining rooms. Everything I see is oversized, ostentatious, and loud. It's overwhelming.

Julian gives Micah and her grandmother a hug, then introduces himself to me. He's delighted to hear about the Florablanca Inn project, and I fill him in on some of the plans we have. Apparently he was the one who handled the sale of the property to Wilhelmina.

"She's a piece of work," he says, laughing. "Good luck with that one."

"She is a handful," I answer with a chuckle.

He takes us through the house, and Ms. Barbara and Micah both carry a notepad and take notes as we walk. They talk prices with Julian on several items and I wander around, trying not to eavesdrop.

A few of the trinkets I find are high-end designer names: Wedgwood, Tiffany & Co., S. Kirk & Son, and so many others I lose track. Room after room after room is like this. It's an impressive collection, especially for the middle of nowhere in south Alabama.

Once we go upstairs, there are six bedrooms packed with old oak, pine, and cherrywood furniture. I follow Micah into one of the bedrooms, where she approaches a heavy sleigh bed with dark finish. She runs her hands along the rough wood and closes her eyes. Then she sits on the bed, flopping down hard on purpose to check its integrity. She lifts the blankets and inspects the joints, then writes comments on her notepad. She stands, rubbing her hands along the footboard another time, then puts her face close to it and examines the finish. It's fascinating to watch her work, and I want her to tell me what she's thinking at every moment.

I approach her from behind and put my hand on top of hers. She smiles only for a moment, then glances down like she's sad. She doesn't pull away, but I notice she catches her breath for a moment before looking up at me with those big, radiant green eyes.

"How are we doing in here?" Julian, clueless, interrupts us, and I pull my hand away.

"Great!" she answers. "If Nana doesn't want this bed, I may have to pull out my own credit card for it."

"Oh, that's a lovely piece," says Julian. "I imagine Garion is going to have a time getting it down those stairs."

"If he says one word in complaint, I'll get Patsy on him," Micah says.

Julian laughs.

I walk out of the room, then continue to wander the house as Ms. Barbara catches up to Micah and they discuss the sleigh bed. There's a bay window with a bench in another room overlooking the west lawn, so I sit for a bit to collect my thoughts. When Micah and her grandmother enter the room, they hardly notice me, so I watch them work.

They are in their own little world, picking up each piece, looking at every detail, feeling every texture, whispering to each other about whether it would be a good fit for their store and who may be interested in buying it. We're here for hours, so long that Julian offers us sweet tea and sandwiches. Ms. Barbara says she wants a glass of sweet tea, but Micah slaps her hand and tells Julian to give her water. Micah is like a little mother to her own grandmother. It's cute.

It'd be a shame if she never has kids. She'd be a great mom.

And, once again, I'm back in the headspace where I'm agonizing about our age difference. I'm so far ahead of myself I'm choking on my own dust.

We go back down the grand staircase, and Micah and her grandmother sit at the dining room table to review numbers and make final decisions on what they'll purchase. Julian and I step outside and sit in the rocking chairs on the front porch. Even though it's sweltering hot, the sun is going down behind the house, so we're in the shade. He asks me where I'm from and about my new firm, and we each talk about our kids. He has a grandson in seminary school in Birmingham, so I give him restaurant recommendations for his next trip.

When Micah and Ms. Barbara finally come out, they talk figures with Julian and walk through the house to put a red sticker on the items they're taking.

"Garion will be here shortly to get everything," Micah says. "But the Wedgwood we're taking now."

Micah walks to her car and gets several rolls of bubble wrap, and when she returns I help her carefully wrap the jasperware vases, plates, urns, and planters.

"Nana's crazy about some Wedgwood," she tells me as we roll, tape, and repeat.

"I don't blame her," I say. "You know, the art museum in

Birmingham has the largest Wedgwood collection in North America."

"Really?" she says. "I had no idea."

"You'll have to come up sometime. I'll take you there."

She hesitates, then smiles. "That would be nice."

All of a sudden the front door slams, and we walk into the foyer to see a tall, thin older lady with square shoulders and a crazy mass of white hair standing by the door like she owns the place. For a moment, I wonder if it's the ghost of the former owner. She's wearing all black, but there are sequins covering her loose shirt and pants. She has a ring on every finger and enough necklaces to make Lil' Wayne jealous. She almost reminds me of Ruth, the lady I met at Finnegan House, only wilder and unhinged, even feral.

"Pauline," says Julian in an accusatory tone, "what are you doing here?"

"There's an estate sale tomorrow," she says.

"That's right," he answers. "Tomorrow. Not today."

"Well, I wanted a sneak peek. Hello, Barbara."

Micah's grandmother steps out of the sitting room with a look of amusement. "Causing trouble again, Pauline?" she asks.

"No trouble. Just nosy. You know that old bitch never let anyone in, and we all knew she was loaded."

Ms. Barbara shakes her head with a smirk. Micah, wide-eyed and ghost-white, and gives me an uncomfortable look.

"Oh, look at this!" Pauline says, picking up a silver tray

etched with swans. "I need this. Did you already buy it, Barb?"

"No, it's all yours."

She tucks it under her arm. "Got any jewelry?" she asks Julian.

"You can find out tomorrow when the sale opens to the public."

"Tsk. I don't want people touching my things with their grubby little hands."

"They aren't your things, Pauline," says Julian.

"There's jewelry upstairs in the bedroom," Ms. Barbara says. Julian shoots her a look. She winks at him as Pauline makes her way upstairs.

"Barbara, what are you trying to do to me?" Julian asks once the woman disappears. "She's gonna walk out with half the stuff and not pay me a dime."

"Oh, she's just airing out her crazy."

Julian shakes his head and follows Pauline up the stairs.

"Who is that?" I ask once they're out of earshot.

"A lunatic," says Micah.

"Pauline and I went to high school together," explains Ms. Barbara. "She came from money, married more money, and has never had anything but time on her hands. It's made her a little eccentric."

"She digs up city flowerbeds for fun, and she once chased Patsy's mama down the road with an ax."

I feel my eyes bug out of my head. "I'm sorry. What?"

"Yeah, their cat was pooping in her yard. First, she tried to catch the cat and decapitate it, but when Patsy's mama came outside, she went after her instead."

"Did she go to jail?"

"No. The police told her they can't do anything about Pauline Cavendish."

I stand there, astonished. I guess even the most charming town has a vein of insanity.

"She always shows up at these estate sales and tries to steal stuff."

"Wow. That's…uh…wow." I'm not really sure what to say.

"She could afford the whole lot," says Ms. Barbara, "but I think she loves giving Julian a hard time. She has nothing else to do."

They finally come back downstairs with a handful of necklaces, the silver tray still tucked under her arm.

"I'll send a check to your office," she tells Julian.

"Okay, Pauline. Be safe getting home."

He tries to lead her to the front door, but she pauses and looks at Micah.

"You're mighty tall," she says, as if surprised. Micah says nothing, but rolls her eyes. "Your mama ever get herself straightened out?"

Micah shoots a look to her grandmother, who shakes her head and shows Pauline out the door.

"Is she gonna pay you for that stuff?" Micah asks Julian after her grandmother and Pauline are on the porch.

"Sometimes she does, sometimes she doesn't. I'm only glad she left. Mercy, that woman has a devil in her."

I stand there in astonishment and catch Micah staring at me with a grin on her face.

"Welcome to south Alabama," she says.

We drive home mostly in silence, and I'm trying to figure out how I'm going to ask Micah on a date tonight.

When we're inside the city limits, she finally speaks.

"Did you see that Pauline took the necklace I wanted?" she asks her grandmother.

"I did," she says. "But jewelry wasn't on our list."

"I know, but I wanted it for me."

"What was it?" I ask.

"Oh, it was beautiful. An art deco piece with emeralds. Looked like something straight out of The Great Gatsby."

"It was pretty," says Ms. Barbara. "And expensive."

"She'll probably throw it in a drawer and never look at it again."

"Well, one day she'll die and we'll be at her estate sale," Ms. Barbara says. Her tone is so casual it's humorous. "You'll get a second shot at it."

"Evil never dies," says Micah.

"Does she have kids?" I ask.

"No," says Ms. Barbara.

"Proof there is a God," chimes in Micah. "She would've been a horrid mother."

I remember the comment Pauline made about Micah's own mother, but keep my curiosity to myself.

We pull into the hotel, and Micah parks by my car.

"Rhodes, are you staying another night?" she asks.

"Yes, I am."

"Well, if you don't have dinner plans, Micah can take you—"

"Nana, I have plans," she says. I pause midway while opening the car door. I guess that takes care of my asking-Micah-out dilemma.

"Oh! What are you doing?" I ask, dreading the answer. She probably has dates lined up for the next few months.

"I'm going to Montgomery."

Ms. Barbara says nothing, only shakes her head.

"Well, another time. Rhodes, you know, I don't have your card. Can you give it to me so we can be in touch about the fountain?"

"Yes, ma'am," I say, reaching into my wallet and retrieving one for her. She's in the front seat so I can't see what she's doing.

"Here," she says, handing me an old receipt with a phone number on the back. "That's Micah's number. If you need anything, call her. She's better at these gadgets than I am." She waves her phone around like it's a toy, then gives me a wink.

Thank God for Ms. Barbara.

Though now I'm wondering what Micah has going on tonight. My gut tells me she has a date, and my heart sinks. I'm probably competing with ten other guys.

"It was a wonderful day," I say. "Thank you so much for letting me tag along."

They each say goodbye, and the thick evening air greets me as soon as I exit the car. I'm halfway to the hotel door when I hear Micah's voice call me from behind. I turn, and she's trotting towards me, her red hair bouncing over her shoulders.

"I'm sorry if Nana made that awkward."

"No, don't apologize. I should've gotten your number weeks ago when we had lunch. I clearly needed a little help." I chuckle, a bit embarrassed. "I was planning to ask you to dinner anyway, but since you have plans..."

Her face drops. "I'm sorry. It's something I can't get out of. Next time you're here, though, I'd love to go to dinner with you."

Relief floods my body, and I already can't wait to come back.

"You have my number now, so stay in touch," she says.

"I absolutely will," I say. She gives me a hug, and when I wrap my arms around her, I don't want to let go. She's tall enough I don't have to bend over, and she smells like lavender and vanilla. I want to kiss her, but I know her grandmother is watching from the car.

She lets go, and I watch her walk away. I wave as their car leaves the parking lot, then go back to the emptiness of my hotel room.

MICAH

After we leave Rhodes at the hotel, Nana and I ride home in silence. I must admit I'm having mixed feelings about seeing Garrett tonight. Maybe I should stay home and have dinner with Rhodes instead. That's certainly what Nana wants, and I'm positive my friends would feel the same way.

Once we get home, I get a text from Garion—he's on his way to meet Julian at the house to pick up the pieces we bought. He's going to put them in the old rectory for now, and once Nana and I decide which pieces to have in the store, he'll help us get it all moved.

I don't have time to wash my hair, so I put it in a shower cap and rinse the sticky day off my body before driving to Montgomery. I reapply my makeup, fix my hair by re-curling the ends and spraying some dry shampoo in the front, and return to my bedroom in my robe to pick out an outfit. I decide on a seafoam green sweater with a deep v-neck, bootcut jeans to hide my calves, and gladiator sandals.

Before I leave, I make sure Nana has dinner lined up, lay out her medication for her, and give her a kiss on the cheek.

The sun has set by the time I hit the road, and on the drive I get a text from Garion with a photo of his packed-out moving truck with all our stuff from the house. This only makes me think of Rhodes, and I find myself driving a little slower on the back roads to Montgomery.

I arrive at Garrett's apartment and sit in the car for a few moments before going in. Part of me doesn't even want to be here, which is new for me, and I'm not sure what to do. He lives alone on the third floor in a scantily-decorated one-bedroom unit. I've offered to help him fix it up, but that seemed to freak him out, so I haven't brought it up again.

When I finally go up, he greets me at the front door, wearing a plain white t-shirt with jeans and bare feet. He's my height, thin, and has light, messy hair. The apartment smells amazing—like onions, peppers, and garlic.

"I'm making us tacos!" he says after giving me a hug.

"Delicious!"

He kisses me, and though I kiss him back, I notice he tastes like beer and cigarettes. I didn't know he smoked, or at least I'd never noticed it before, but I don't say anything.

He offers me a drink, which I take. I follow him to the harshly-lit kitchen and he talks about his day. Apparently he had to lay off some of his people due to performance, and he's hoping he can replace them soon since they have some big contracts coming up. I nod and listen, offering empathy where I can.

He talks about his brother and sister-in-law expecting another baby, and his other brother, who recently got engaged. Apparently this makes his parents anxious for him to settle down, but he doesn't understand why he has to conform, especially since he's married to his work. The whole conversation makes me sad, not to mention bored out of my mind. I really should've chosen dinner with Rhodes.

I look around the apartment as I listen to him drone. Sistine does have a point. This is not the living space of someone with a successful company. Most of the time, he looks like he just wandered out of a used video game store, not a boardroom. Maybe it is all a lie. Maybe he even believes it.

As we eat dinner, I have another beer and limit myself to one taco so my stomach isn't too full. He continues to talk about himself, and for the first time, I notice he never asks about me. I know I've told him about Nana and her health problems, but not once has he expressed any interest in how she's doing, or how things are going at the store.

After dinner, we go to the bedroom and put on a movie, but don't watch it. When he kisses me, he still tastes like stale beer, and his hands are so clumsy trying to get my clothes off that I almost leave. I feel like I'm going through the motions and, if I'm honest with myself, I don't want to be here. I don't know why I stay.

Once it's over I put on my clothes, get my purse, and he walks me to the door.

"Thank you for driving up here, babe. It was so great to see you again."

"Yeah. Take care, Garrett."

He kisses me and I walk away.

He has no awareness of how disconnected I've been throughout this entire evening. He doesn't care either way. I normally feel exhilarated and giddy when I leave him, but tonight I only feel sadness—partly for him, but mostly for myself.

This is not what I want.

Maybe I do deserve better.

RHODES

I think about going to Cattywampus, but I feel weird being the lone guy at the bar, especially in a place where everyone knows everyone else. So, after spending a lonely night in my hotel room eating Big Ol' Butts BBQ take-out again, I drive back to Birmingham at the crack of dawn.

I keep obsessing over whether Micah had a date last night. It was probably with someone younger who is closer to where she is in life. Someone without gray hair or a son in grad school. Someone who could give her a future with kids, PTA meetings, the whole nine yards.

Once I get to my loft, I text my son to check in, then dig Micah's number out of my bag. I program it into my phone, then type her a message.

Hi Micah, it's Rhodes. I made it home to Bham. I hope you have fun plans for the holiday weekend. Let me know if you want to meet up next time I'm in Magnolia Row.

It's Labor Day weekend. The city should be relatively

quiet, with most people going to the beach or lake houses to celebrate before the funky fall weather sets in.

I sit on the cold leather couch without turning on the television and stare at my phone. I'd forgotten how insecure dating makes a person.

Finally, my phone dings. It's my son. He assures me he's doing well and doesn't need anything. He's going to Lake Martin for the weekend with some of his friends from undergrad, and agrees to meet me for dinner on Monday on his way back through town.

I leave the phone on the coffee table and unpack my bag. I'm starting a load of laundry when I hear another message come through. Like a schoolboy with a crush, I drop what I'm doing and run to check it. I get butterflies when I see Micah's name.

Hey! I forgot it was a holiday weekend! No plans yet, but I'll see what my girlfriends are up to. Glad you made it back home okay. And yes, let me know next time you're in town. I'd love to do dinner or something.

Part of me wants to be nosy and ask her how last night went, but the other part of me doesn't want to know. At least she mentioned hanging out with her girlfriends specifically, which tells me she doesn't have plans with whoever my competition may be.

And—the best part—she wants to see me again.

I respond that I'll let her know as soon as I make plans to head back her way.

Once I finish getting my laundry going, I make a grocery list, head to the store, and come home with enough food to ensure I won't have to leave until it's time to meet my son for dinner on Monday. I settle on the couch, turn on college football, grab my briefcase, and dig out the photo album from the museum in Magnolia Row.

I'm flipping through the pages, examining each photo meticulously to make sure I haven't missed anything, when something in a photo of the lobby catches my eye. Right above the fountain in the lobby is an elegant line of crystals hanging from the ceiling. If I had to guess, it's the bottom section of a massive chandelier that once graced the thirty-foot space in the entry.

I take a picture of it and text Micah, asking if she knows what happened to it. She responds quickly, saying she doesn't but her grandmother can check into it. I thank her, then settle back into a quiet weekend alone.

$\mathcal{M}$onday night finally rolls around after a lonely weekend and I'm meeting my son at Tasty Town for dinner. He looks good, not too stressed yet, though it is only his first semester of law school. We order hummus and entrees and he tells me about his professors, trying to develop new study habits to keep up, and his anxieties about moot court.

"What about you, Dad? The new firm going well?"

I tell him about Magnolia Row, the hotel, and even Micah and her grandmother. He's smiling the whole time I'm talking.

"What is it?" I ask. "You're grinning ear to ear."

"I haven't seen you this excited about anything since… well, since ever."

"That's not true. I've been excited for everything you've done."

"Not like this. You're so animated today. It's a nice change, even if it is a little strange."

"Thank you, I guess."

"Are you seeing someone?" he asks, which completely comes out of the blue. He's never once asked me about my love life. I'm taken aback and fidget with my almost-empty water glass while trying to think of what to say.

"Sorry to pry," he says. "You never talk about it. I thought it may explain why you're so happy all of a sudden."

"Well, this project is the biggest thing I've worked on in a long time, and it's coming together really nicely. It's everything I wanted to do when I quit my job. But, if I'm being honest, the girl who owns the antique shop with her grandmother…. Well, she's special."

Mason's face lit up. "So you do have a girlfriend?"

"No, no, no. We had one lunch date and said we'd see each other next time I'm in town. It's very early. While I do like her, I have some reservations."

"Like what?"

This feels like an out-of-body experience. I never thought I'd talk to my son about dating. Ever.

"She's younger. She's only thirty. Hell, she's closer to your age than mine." I sigh and run my fingers through my hair. "I'm still trying to wrap my head around it."

"If she likes you, and you're on the same page, it shouldn't matter."

Somehow, hearing the validation from Mason calms my anxiety like a blanket on a fire. Having his stamp of approval is everything to me.

"Maybe you're right. We'll see where it goes. It's still early."

"Well," says Mason, "I want to see this hotel when it's done. It sounds incredible."

"It will be, yes."

We eat dinner, talk sports, and he gets back in his car to drive to Tuscaloosa. I stand in the empty street and watch his taillights disappear. It's a strange thing when your child becomes your peer, but I wouldn't trade it for the world. He's my best friend.

I return to my loft, trying to think of a reason to text Micah, but fall asleep before coming up with anything.

That night, I dream of dancing with her in the sparkling ballroom of the Florablanca Inn.

MICAH

For the entire week after Labor Day, Nana and I are busy rearranging the store and cataloguing everything we bought the week before. Patsy's husband Garion and his brother had to come on Wednesday after hours to help me move and reassemble some of the heavier pieces, and by Friday, we have a packed store full of new-to-us items.

I've only had brief texts with Garrett since I saw him in Montgomery. If I'm being honest with myself, I much prefer the company of the definitely-successful, intelligent, sexy architect over the insecure, who-knows-if-he-even-has-a-real-job, boring computer guy.

When I take a step back and compare the two, it's comical. There is no comparison. Rhodes is leaps and bounds better than Garrett. The problem is I still don't feel like I'm good enough for him, and it makes me uncomfortable. He could get any thin, confident, educated girl he wants. Why would he want me?

I'm walking through the store with my phone, recording a video to show off our new products on social media, when I catch Nana standing in her office door, giving me an amused look.

"You know the chandelier you asked about?"

"For Rhodes?"

"That's the one. I called Julian since I figured he would know what happened to it."

"And?"

"You're never going to guess who has it."

My heart sinks. "Pauline."

Nana laughs. "The one and only."

"Well, so much for that."

"No, I think if we go over there—"

"Nana, I am NOT going to Pauline Cavendish's house."

"Why not?"

"Because I don't want to die."

"Oh, she's harmless."

I make a face. She knows the stories about that crazy old bat better than I do.

"Well, maybe not always," Nana continues, "but I can handle her."

I shake my head. "I'll let Rhodes know."

I text Rhodes to let him know we found the chandelier, and he says he'll be in town next Friday to see it. We make plans for dinner, which sends butterflies all through my gut.

At least I have a week to plan my outfit.

*T*hat night I meet Kendall, Sistine, and Patsy at Cattywampus. We get our usual high top in the center of the room where we have a good 360-degree view of everyone and everything for optimal gossip.

"Soooo," says Patsy, looking at me. "What's the latest on SAM?"

"Who?" I ask. It's a common enough name, but I still don't know a Sam.

"Sexy Architect Man!" She gives me a huge smile, showing off the adorable little gap between her two front teeth.

"Seriously?" I ask.

"Patsy's been calling him that in our group chat," says Sistine.

"What group chat? I haven't seen this."

"The one we have to talk about you and your love life behind your back," says Patsy.

"She wasn't supposed to know about it," says Sistine.

"This is all very enlightening," I say. "It must be a boring thread."

"Garion said SAM was with you and your Nana at an estate sale last week."

"Well, yes, but—"

"He's spending time with Nana too!" says Kendall. "That's promising! Does she like him?"

"She loves him, but that's not—"

"Have you gone out again?"

"No. He asked me out, but I had plans with Garrett."

They all slump back in their chairs and look at me like I'm a moron. I can't disagree with them.

"What?"

"You turned down a date with Sexy Architect Man for a loser who uses you when it's convenient for him?" asks Patsy.

"He didn't stand you up this time, did he?" asks Sistine.

"No, I saw him."

My face must've fallen, because Kendall reaches out and grabs my arm. "Are you okay, Micah?" she asks in her sweet Kendall way. "You look so sad."

"I'm fine, it's just… I don't know. I'm getting bored with Garrett."

"Praise Jesus!" says Patsy, loud enough the people at the table next to us turn to stare.

"What about SAM?" asks Kendall.

"His name is Rhodes."

"Whatever," says Sistine. "Are you seeing him again?"

"Yes, Nana made sure we exchanged numbers."

"Thank God for Nana," says Patsy.

I roll my eyes at her. "We're going to go out a week from tonight when he's back in town."

Patsy squeals, again drawing attention to our table, and Kendall claps like I won the lottery.

"Micah," says Sistine in all seriousness, "don't freak out and get insecure on him. You deserve to be happy. If he's going to treat you well and go out of his way to get to know you, be open to it. If he's asking you out, he obviously thinks you're good enough."

Damn her. She knew what I was thinking without me saying a word.

"I'll try. I promise."

Rhodes meets Nana and me at the store a week later to ride to Pauline's house. He's as handsome as ever, hands in his pockets and bright-eyed as the morning sun. He's had a haircut, which only makes the angles of his face look more pronounced and masculine. And he smells like Adonis. I swear I could get drunk on him. Nana gives him a hug and tells him as much.

We take Rhodes' car since he offers to drive, and I let Nana have the front seat so I can admire him from behind. She directs him to Pauline's massive Greek revival house a few blocks off Magnolia Row's main historic district. The azaleas in front are unkempt and the grass hasn't been cut in ages, but it's easy to see the former majesty of the house.

Shame it's home to an absolute witch.

"She knows we're coming, right?" I ask as we get out of the car.

"No, she doesn't have a phone," says Nana. She closes the car door and approaches the house like she's expected.

Rhodes has a worried look, and I grab his arm as we walk behind Nana. "We're gonna die!" I whisper, and he chuckles before putting his hand on mine.

Nana ascends the stairs onto the wide front porch and rings the doorbell. Then we wait.

And wait.

She rings again, then goes to peer in the floor-length windows. Apparently seeing someone, she waves. A moment later, Pauline is at the door. She's fully dressed in what looks like shiny silver pajamas, which sets off her white hair. Her face is full of gaudy makeup, and she's wearing even more jewelry than she was the day she showed up at the estate sale. She's holding a cocktail and is clearly drunk.

"Barbara Bonaventure. What the hell are you doing here?" she asks, one arm above her head as she leans on the door.

"Good to see you again, Pauline. We were wondering about something you bought a while back. Can we come in?"

"No. Tell Julian I'll send him a check when I'm ready to."

"We're not here for Julian," says Nana. "It's about an item from the old hotel by the river."

"Oh yes, the Florablanca Inn. I heard some out-of-town money bought it up."

"They did," says Nana. "You remember Rhodes from the other day? He's the architect overseeing the restoration."

Pauline turns her attention to Rhodes, looking at him like she hadn't noticed him standing there until this moment.

"You were at the estate sale."

"I was, yes."

"What do you want with me?" she asks, suddenly taking

interest. "You know, I haven't had a man—" She starts to walk towards him, but Nana grabs her hand.

"He's here on business, Pauline. Julian said you bought the chandelier that was in the hotel lobby."

"I did."

"Do you still have it?" asks Rhodes.

"I reckon I do somewhere."

"You don't know?" I ask. How can you not know if or where you have an entire chandelier?

She looks at me and stares. "That's none of your business, girl."

I roll my eyes.

"Pauline," says Nana, "we're looking to buy it from you so it can go back into the hotel."

She takes a sip of her drink and tilts her head back. "It won't be cheap."

"My client has deep pockets," says Rhodes.

"Come on, then. It's out back, but we'll have to go through the house since the fence fell."

We follow her through the house, stopping to retrieve a set of hidden keys from a hallway buffet table. It smells like rotten plants and old perfume. A thick layer of dust covers almost everything, and the rooms are more packed than the ones at the estate sale a few weeks ago.

"Sorry about the mess," she says. "My maid quit on me about twenty years back."

"I can't imagine why," I say under my breath. Rhodes hears me and puts a finger to his lips.

We reach to the back porch, which is covered in old furniture that's warped and rotten from being exposed to the weather. I shake my head. A lot of these pieces were probably beautiful at some point.

"Watch out for snakes," Pauline says as we navigate the weeds.

Once we get to the carriage house at the back of the property, Pauline unlocks the door but is unable to open it due to the underbrush. Rhodes steps forward to help, kicking the weeds back while pulling on the decaying wood slab until it's finally ajar enough for us to slip inside.

The carriage house is in even worse shape than the main house. An old Mercedes convertible is parked on the left side, but the top has been eaten through and the interior has started to rot. Countless paintings and vintage mirrors are leaning against the walls, and an open chifforobe reveals moldy, tattered clothing. It reeks of must and decay, and I can't help but cover my face with my cardigan to keep from breathing in the dust and mold.

Once my eyes adjust to the dim light, I see on the right side of the room, opposite the car, a huge lump covered in a dirty white sheet. Pauline, still nursing her cocktail, grabs a corner and tries to pull it back, but it catches. Rhodes motions for her to step back, and I help him carefully remove the sheet to reveal the chandelier.

It's resting at a catty-corner angle, but it's still striking. It's tiered like a wedding cake, and each layer has elegant looping arms curling up to hold the candle-shaped lights. Hundreds, if not thousands, of crystals adorn every inch of the piece, and even in this dark, awful space, it's easy to appreciate how beautiful it once was. I look at Rhodes, whose face is alight as he stares open-mouthed.

"Pauline, why did you buy this if you were just going to hide it back here?" Nana asks.

"Ruth Cottar wanted it for Finnegan House." Nana rolls her eyes as Pauline continues. "I really hate that bitch."

"Well, if you're willing to part with it, my client would absolutely want to purchase it from you."

"Good luck getting it out," she says.

Rhodes takes some photos with his phone and we follow Nana and Pauline back to the main house.

"Y'all want a cocktail?" Pauline asks when we get back into the air conditioning.

"Better not," says Nana. "We have to get back to the store."

"How can I reach you about the chandelier?" asks Rhodes.

"Well, I'm always here," she says, as if the notion of reaching her by phone or email is simply ridiculous. "Besides, gives you a reason to come back and let me have another look at you."

He smiles politely as we leave.

I drop off Micah and her grandmother back at their store, then check in at the Mossy River Motel. I pull up my email, send photos of the chandelier to Wilhelmina and the rest of my team, then search online find a restoration company in Atlanta that may be able to clean and rewire the massive piece.

After finishing work, I shower, change into a light blue button-down with khakis, and watch ESPN until it's time to pick up Micah.

I'm nervous. I shouldn't be, since I've seen her multiple times. I'm used to being around her at this point, but she's disarming. She's built like a goddess and her mane of red hair drives me insane.

Once the sun goes down, I grab my keys, wallet, and phone, and drive to the home Micah shares with her grandmother. It's a little ways outside of town, set back from the road, with a huge, well-kept yard. It's a typical ranch-style home, popular in the 1960s, and on the front and side porches there are huge hanging ferns swaying in the evening breeze.

I pull into the gravel drive and park by the side porch, as Micah instructed. She opens the sliding glass door and shows me in, and I feel like I've immediately stepped back into the late 60s or early 70s. The carpet is a brown, orange, and yellow shag that is probably older than Moses. The kitchen has the original Frigidaire puke-green enamel appliances and little mushroom-painted canisters on the counter. Doilies are on every table surface, including the dining room table, which has a huge lace tablecloth with orange placemats.

It reminds me of my own grandparents' home outside of Birmingham and makes me miss them. It's strange how nostalgia can hit at the most unexpected times.

But as charming as the house is, Micah nearly takes my breath away. She's wearing a low-cut black shirt that's tight on her chest paired with loud jewelry: peacock feather earrings with a matching lariat necklace and an emerald cocktail ring.

Ms. Barbara, wrapped in an afghan, sits in an oversized recliner that swallows her. I lean over and give her a kiss on the cheek, which makes her blush.

"Nana, you have plenty of frozen dinners in there, so are you good for tonight?" Micah asks, handing her a cock-tail of medication to take. Her grandmother downs them with a big gulp of ice water.

"Oh, I'm fine," she says. "You kids have fun."

"I won't be out late," Micah tells her, leaning to give her a hug. "I love you."

"Love you too, sugar bug."

My heart swells. I wish my grandmother were still here. She and Ms. Barbara would get along great.

Micah grabs her purse from the side table by the door, and I slide back the glass to let her out.

"Goodnight, Ms. Barbara!" I say, then she winks at me as we turn to leave.

On the ride into town, we talk and laugh about Pauline and all the crazy stuff in her house.

"Did you see the gator head?" I ask her.

"No! Where was it?"

"In the sitting room. It had fake apples in its mouth and a rosary curled between its eyes."

She gave me a belly laugh as loud as it is endearing. "I missed that! The sad thing about her house is she has so much nice stuff, but most of it is in terrible shape. The house itself will probably have to be torn down when she dies."

"Yeah, I was nervous walking through there," I say. "The floor was spongy. I wouldn't be surprised if it falls in on her one day."

"Serves the old bat right. I only hope the antiques don't get damaged."

"Priorities," I chuckle.

"Exactly!" We share a brief glance before I return my eyes to the road.

I could spend every night exactly like this, with her. Riding around, laughing, telling stories. Nothing could be more perfect.

I park in front of the coffee shop and we walk to the

steakhouse. It's packed, so we wait at the bar for a table. I order merlot and Micah gets a Riesling. There's only one barstool available, so I let Micah have it and stand at her side. Luckily, it's a small space and there are so many people I'm forced to be close enough to touch her. I can feel the heat of her body and smell the familiar lavender and vanilla scent she always wears. She's more intoxicating than the wine.

Once our table is ready, we get settled into the corner booth at the back. I order a filet and she gets grilled salmon.

"So how is work going at the hotel?" she asks. "I rode by the other day and it didn't look like anything has started yet."

"No, not yet. We've applied for permits and submitted our plans to the state, so we're waiting for all of that to go through. Since it's a historic property, there's more bureaucracy involved."

"I'm so excited to see it when it's done. I may move in if it's even half as fabulous as I imagine."

"You can be the first guest!" I say, holding my glass up for a toast.

"Absolutely!" She clinks her drink on mine, then leaves a smudge of red lipstick behind after taking a sip.

"I love your house, though. Your grandmother never changes a thing, does she?"

"Nope! Not since she moved in. I think it's because of my grandfather. The house reminds her of him."

"When did he pass?"

"Long before I was born, when my mom was a kid. He had cancer, and it devastated my nana."

"You don't talk about your mom much."

She shifts in her seat, and I know I've struck a nerve. "There's not much to say. She's in and out. Always has been."

"How so?" I ask, worried I'm prying too much, but she doesn't miss a beat.

"Well, she had me when she was a teenager. We lived in a trailer north of town for a few years. Then we moved in with one of her boyfriends, but they broke up. Then we moved in with Nana, which was supposed to be temporary. It was for Mom. She met someone else and left town while I stayed behind. She promised she'd come back and get me once she got settled, but she never did."

"Do you ever see her?"

"When she needs money. If she's between boyfriends, she'll show up under the guise of wanting to help me with Nana, but Nana and I both see through it. Last time she was here, I'm pretty sure she was on something. She would sleep for fourteen to sixteen hours at a time."

"Wow. That's hard, Micah. I'm sorry."

"It's okay. I mean, it's not. But it is what it is, and there's nothing I can do to change it."

"What does your nana say about all of that?"

"She feels guilty. I think when my grandfather died, it gave my mom some issues when it comes to men. Nana feels like she spoiled her too much afterwards."

"You turned out well, though."

"Thanks," she says, looking down.

"What about your dad?" I ask, fidgeting with my napkin.

"No idea. My mom never told anyone who he is, and I suspect she probably doesn't even know herself. Sometimes around town I'll see a man with red hair and wonder, you know?"

"Your mom doesn't have red hair?"

"No, she's a brunette. And short."

"Your Nana is tall, though. I think you look like her."

"Yeah, I get that a lot. I guess I do, except for the hair. She was brunette too before she turned gray. No redheads that we know of on her side, so it must've come from my mystery dad."

"Well, it's a gift. You have the most beautiful hair I've ever seen."

She blushes. "Thank you," she says.

We stare at each other for a few moments, and she looks like she's deep in thought. "What?" I finally ask.

"Honestly?" she asks, and her tone is serious.

"Yeah? Is everything okay?"

"I can't figure out why you're with me."

This completely throws me for a loop. I have no idea what she's talking about.

"What do you mean? If anyone should be asking that question, it's me."

"Seriously?" she asks. "You're gorgeous. You do see the way women in town react to you, don't you? You could have any thin, beautiful, successful woman you want. Especially living in the city. I'm a chunky, awkward, country bumpkin."

I shake my head, completely bumfuzzled. "You're the most stunning woman I've ever seen," I say. "Plus, you're sharp, passionate about the same things I am, and you have the biggest heart in the world. And you're only thirty. I can't figure out why you're out with a middle-aged guy like me."

"You think I'm stunning?" she asked in a small, weak voice.

"Absolutely. You have curves in all the right places, and you carry yourself with such confidence. You're like someone out of an old Hollywood movie."

"You know 'curvy' is usually a euphemism for fat, right?"

My heart sinks. This is not where I wanted this conversation to go. "No, don't say that about yourself. It's not what I meant. Men like women with… you know…" I'm trying not to be crass and mention the voluptuous parts of her body that do it for me, but I suddenly find myself glancing at her chest.

"Your face is bright red," she says, laughing.

I roll my eyes, but I'm happy for the break in tension. "I was trying to not talk about your chest size, but here we are. I apologize."

Dear Lord, this is humiliating. How can a middle-aged man be so bad at talking to women?

"No, it's fine. I'm glad you like me. It's not something I'm used to." I'm relieved by the light tone in her voice, but I can't believe what she's saying.

"Oh come on. I'm sure you've had tons of boyfriends."

"No," she says, her tone flat. "I haven't."

"How is that possible?"

"Well, I have a situationship with this one guy, but it's been years now and it's going nowhere fast, so… yeah. My friends have been telling me since the beginning he was using me, and I'm finally starting to see it for myself."

I nod. I knew there had to be someone else. "I didn't mean to pry."

"It's fine," she says. "I have nothing to hide. Secrets aren't really my style."

"Well, you deserve to be treated like a queen," I say. "Whether it's by me or someone else. Promise me you'll never settle for less."

She nods. "I promise."

"Since we've acknowledged we like each other, there is one thing I want to get out in the open."

"Oh, God. You're not secretly married, are you? I once went out with a guy a few times before finding out he was married, and I felt horrible."

"No, no, no! I've been divorced for quite some time now. But, speaking of being married, you are younger than me. At thirty, you still have plenty of time to start a family. If that's something you want, I'm not your guy. I've already done all of that. I'm in a different phase of life entirely."

She looks surprised.

"Sorry for being so blunt," I continue, "but I don't want you to waste your time, or for us get further down this road and you end up compromising something you want because of me."

"Look, I live day to day taking care of my nana. Even when I go out with guys, I don't ever let myself think too far ahead because it never works out anyway. When it comes to kids, I've never really imagined that for myself."

This surprises me. She gives off so many maternal vibes I can't imagine her not having kids. "Really? Why?"

"I don't know. Maybe because my own mom was so awful it made me never want to be one. Maybe I babysat too many brats when I was a teenager. I'm not sure, but it's never been high on my list of dreams for myself. Besides, I may not even be able to have them. My ovaries are covered in cysts, so it may be difficult regardless of what I want."

"What is on your list of dreams for yourself?" I ask, looking intently into her eyes.

She sighs and sits back in the booth, her gaze trailing off. "I'd love to grow the antique business and maybe open another store in the Mobile area. I want to travel. Learn ballroom dancing."

"Really?" I ask, giving her a look of surprise.

"Absolutely! I watch that dancing show on TV and it looks so fun."

"What else?"

"Well, I don't like to admit it, but I would like someone to share my life with. A partner."

"Why don't you want to admit that?"

"I don't know. I guess I've never felt like it was going to happen, and I didn't want to be disappointed if I ended up alone."

"And now?"

Micah bites her lower lip for a moment. "Now, maybe I can see myself having that with you." She says it almost like a question, squirming in her seat like a nervous kid.

"Same," I say. "I'd love to share all of that with you."

She tilts her head to the side, like she's thinking of what to say next. "Rhodes, I really like you," she finally says. "You're the best man I've ever gone out with. I'd like to see where this is going. I'm not worried about your age, or kids, or any of that right now. Besides, age is just a number."

"Well," I say, "I'll concede if you agree your size is also just a number, and it's one I have absolutely no concern about. You are perfect as you are." I know I've struck a nerve, because her eyes start to water.

"No one has ever talked to me like this before."

"Like what? Kindly?"

"Yes," she says in all earnestness, nodding her head. "Not a guy, anyway. I'm never the girl a guy wants to settle down with."

I reach across the table and grab her hands in mine. Her face softens and she rubs her thumbs across my knuckles. I wish I could stop time and save this moment forever.

Our perfect, beautiful connection is interrupted by our food arriving. It smells delicious, and we order one more round of drinks before digging in. Once we start eating, I change the subject and tell her about all the steps we have in the restoration and fill her in on some other prospective projects I have all over the South.

"Hopefully the next several months will be busy," I say.

"How long do you think it'll take for the hotel to be finished?" she asks.

"We're looking at a year and a half, weather depending. The biggest thing is going to be fixing the foundation on the east wing. We basically have to remove a massive wooden beam from the bottom of the structure, hold the building up, and replace it without the side of the hotel falling off."

"After that, you're done with Magnolia Row?"

Now I get where she's going with her questioning. "Not if I have a reason to stay," I answer, and she smiles.

MICAH

I've been on dozens of dates with douchebags I met online, yet not one of them ever made my stomach do cartwheels the way Rhodes does.

After we finish dinner, I go to the restroom and rinse my mouth with a little bottle of mouthwash I'd put in my purse in case the night ends in kisses.

And it definitely will. I can't believe how well this date is going.

Before I walk out of the restroom, I check myself in the full-length mirror by the door. No, I'm not the skinny stick-figure model type. But I guess if a guy likes big booties and boobies, I have them in spades.

I haven't felt this confident in, well, ever. I'd like to think my self-worth and confidence are not influenced by a guy, but it does make a difference when someone like Rhodes looks at me like he wants to scoop me up and kiss me until my entire being is nothing but warmth and happiness. It's a nice change.

We leave the restaurant and he drives me home. I'm so nervous, and I hope he kisses me this time. I'd wanted him to kiss me after our lunch date, and many times since, but there were always people around. It's after eight o'clock now, so Nana should be in bed. That'll give us some privacy.

Or so I thought.

When we pull up to the house, I'm not surprised to see the outside flood lights blazing, as Nana always leaves them on when I'm gone, but I am surprised to see light coming from most of the windows in the house. She always turns off the interior lights before going to bed.

"That's odd," I say to Rhodes. "Surely she's not still awake."

"We'll check it out," says Rhodes, with a slight edge in his voice.

He parks by the side door and my heart drops when I look through the glass. The kitchen, living room, hall, and bedroom lights are on, and I see Nana's arm stretched across the floor between the dining room and kitchen.

I scream, fumble to get my keys and throw back the door before rushing to my nana, who is breathing but disoriented.

"I'm calling an ambulance," Rhodes says. He kneels at my side.

"Tell them to hurry. She has diabetes and heart disease," I say, clutching my grandmother. I give the address to Rhodes, who relays it to the dispatcher.

"Grab her medicine," I say. "I keep it all in the box by the stove."

He retrieves it, puts it on the counter by his keys, and sits with me on the floor while I rock my nana and beg her not to die. The surreal moment blurs with a million jumbled thoughts in my head. I feel like I'm choking on my own breath. She feels so frail in my arms that it scares me.

"I'm not ready for this," I whisper to Rhodes, who stays calm and rubs my back, telling me over and over it's all going to be okay.

I've never been so scared in my life. My heart is racing and an overwhelming sense of dread makes me feel heavy and nauseous.

This cannot be happening. I can't live without my nana.

It seems like forever until the paramedics arrive, but once they're here, they take over and get her onto a stretcher. She's still not coherent, but she moans and bobs her head when they try to talk to her.

At least she's alive, I think, clutching Rhodes' hand like my life depends on it.

While they're lifting her onto the gurney, I search the kitchen for signs of whether she ate. There are no dishes in the sink, no empty containers in the trash can.

Rhodes watches me with a look of concern. "I gave her insulin before we left," I say. "I don't think she ate dinner. And she barely touched her lunch earlier. She's in shock."

Once the paramedics take her out of the house, they tell me I can ride with them to the local hospital.

"I'll follow behind," says Rhodes, picking up the box of medication.

He meets me behind the ambulance, giving me a kiss on

the forehead and a hug before I climb in behind my grandmother. It calms me and lets me know I'm not alone.

The first few hours at the hospital are a blur. Rhodes, as promised, follows behind us and meets me in the parking lot. He gives the box of medication to the nurse so they can see what she's taking, and I fill out paperwork while we wait in the lobby. The harsh light and smell of cleaner makes me feel sick, and once I return Nana's information to the front desk, I fight the urge to lay down on the floor and cry.

I don't know what I'd do without Rhodes here. We sit next to each other on the cold peach-colored chairs, and he puts his arm around me.

"She'll be okay," he says over and over again. I want so badly to believe it's true.

The doctor comes out after what feels like ages and confirms my suspicions. She went into shock from not eating enough and may have even had a seizure. Her blood pressure is also high, so they're keeping her for a few days. But for the moment, she is stable.

I break down and my entire body goes limp. If Rhodes wasn't here to hold me as I cry, I would've been on the floor.

The doctor says they're moving her to a room and once she's settled, they'll let me see her. He walks away as I focus on my breathing to calm myself as Rhodes rubs my back.

"I should've taken better care of her," I say. "This is my fault. I shouldn't have gone with you until I made sure she ate. Or at least I should've checked her blood sugar before we left."

"No, Micah. You can't blame yourself. She's old and fragile."

I shake my head. "I should've been there," I whisper.

He puts his arm around me and squeezes tight. He doesn't let go until the nurse comes to let us know we can see Nana.

When we enter, her eyes are closed and she looks like she's aged ten years in the past few hours. The room is freezing and smells like bleach, and I can't help but notice how austere everything looks. My nana doesn't belong in a place like this.

"There's my sugar bug," she says, opening her eyes when she hears us approach. Her voice is scratchy and thin.

"Nana, I'm so sorry," I say, leaning in to give her a tight hug.

"Oh, it's nothing," she says. "I'm alright. Don't you worry your pretty little head about me."

"I always worry about you," I say.

"You shouldn't make a fuss over an old lady like me," she says, her voice weak. "Rhodes," she says, holding a hand out towards him. He takes it and places his other hand on top of hers. "I apologize for ruining your date."

"I'm glad you're okay," he says.

"You didn't ruin it, Nana," I whisper.

"Go on home, now. Let me get some sleep."

I don't want to leave, but I know I'll keep her up if I stay. Besides, the doctor had assured me she's stable.

I give her another hug and tell her I love her and I'll see her tomorrow—which is actually today. My sense of time is completely out of whack. We stop in the hallway to talk to the nurses, then Rhodes and I leave the hospital.

When we walk outside, the sun is rising. We drive back to my house in silence.

"Are you going back to Birmingham today?" I ask him when we pull into the driveway.

"I don't have to," he says. "Do you want me to stay?"

"Yes. I mean, I need to sleep and collect myself. I'll see Nana later today, but maybe afterwards we can do something."

"Sounds perfect," he says. He walks me to the door and gives me a long, tight hug. I never want him to let go. I feel so safe, so secure in his arms, and I want it to last forever. He kisses me on the forehead, then loosens his grip.

"Let me know if you need anything," he says.

"I will. Thank you."

I slide open the door, realizing I neglected to lock it when we went to the hospital. After I step inside, I turn to see Rhodes walking to his car.

Part of me wants to ask him to stay, but it feels like too much, too soon. This is all too heavy considering we've technically only been on two dates.

Every light in the house is still on, so I turn them off and go to the bathroom to wash my face and brush my teeth. When I look in the mirror, I frighten myself. Last night's makeup is now under my eyes, my face is swollen and red from crying, and my hair is disheveled like I'd been sleeping for a week. I can't believe Rhodes saw me like this.

I push the thought away. I can't think about that now. I go to my room, take off my clothes, and crash.

RHODES

When I get back to the hotel, I talk to the girl in the lobby about extending my stay for one more night—which is no issue since this place is always half-empty—then go to my room and collapse. I've been up for nearly twenty-four hours at this point, and my whole body hurts.

But it was worth it to be there for Micah. I'm so glad she wasn't alone. My heart ached for her in those hours at the hospital. It was excruciating to watch, but I wouldn't have had it any other way.

I sit on the edge of the bed, take off my shoes, and sit for a moment, staring into the beige nothingness of the floral wallpaper. It's almost as if I'm too tired to sleep, so I go into a trance. I take a deep breath to snap myself out of it, then take off the rest of my clothes and crawl under the covers.

I'm asleep as soon as my head hits the pillow.

When I wake, it's lunchtime. My stomach howls and I'm desperate for coffee. I check my phone, but Micah hasn't reached out. I send her a quick text, letting her know I'm thinking about her and to let me know if she needs anything.

I take a quick shower, put on the extra set of clothes I thankfully brought, and go to Main Street to Bonny Beans Coffee Shop. I recognize the girl behind the counter as one of Micah's friends.

"Hey, SAM," she says when I get to the register.

I turn to make sure no one else is behind me. "You must have me mistaken—"

"No, I don't. You're Sexy Architect Man."

I raise my eyebrows and stare at her. This is awkward.

"I'm Micah's friend. That's what we've been calling you in our group text. SAM."

I smile and nod, unsure whether to be embarrassed or flattered. "Yes, I'm the architect."

"Speaking of Micah," the girl says. "I got a text from our friend Patsy. She said her car wasn't at the antique store this morning and it looks like the place hasn't opened. She's not answering our texts. Is everything okay?"

"No." I tell her about Ms. Barbara and our night at the hospital.

"I'm glad you were there for her," she says, her eyes wide and brows furrowed in concern. "Coffee's on me, whatever you want."

I order a latte with double espresso and a bagel. She makes it for me, then disappears into the kitchen with her phone.

Once I finish eating, I wave goodbye to Sistine and return to the hotel. Part of me wants to go to the hospital to check on Micah's grandmother myself, but I also want to give her the space she needs. So, I wait.

A few hours later, she texts me and asks me to pick her up at her house at eight o'clock. I breathe a sigh of relief. If she's wanting to go out tonight, it must mean her grandmother is doing better.

When I arrive at her house, she's waiting for me on the patio with a small backpack. Her face is still puffy and I notice it's also free of the make-up she normally wears. Her hair is pulled back in a high, bouncy ponytail, like one of those vintage Barbie dolls. She's also more casually dressed in wide-leg jeans and a Cattywampus Brewing t-shirt.

"Sorry I look like a ragamuffin," she says. "I figured after you saw me at my worst last night, you could probably handle me without all the fixins."

"You're beautiful regardless," I say, giving her a hug.

She looks in my eyes. "Wow," she says. "You really mean that."

"Of course I do," I answer. I almost kiss her there in the porch light, but she pulls back and tells me she has a surprise for me.

We get in my car and drive back towards town, down Main Street and past the brewery in the direction of the old Victorian Village. As we drive, she tells me her grandmother is doing—and looking—much better since we left her at the hospital early this morning. Micah spent most of the afternoon there, and apparently after I told Sistine what was going on, her friends showed up to visit as well.

I'm glad she had the support, and the fact that she has such devoted friends speaks volumes. I respect the hell out of it.

Streetlights stop after we pass the Florablanca Inn, which looks like something out of a horror movie at night, so the path is dark and there are no cars or signs of life. Micah points out the cemetery where she and her friends would hang out in high school. It's old, with an iron fence, leaning headstones, and Spanish moss hanging low enough to touch the ground. You'd have to go to Salem to find a spookier place.

Past the cemetery, she tells me to slow down. She leans forward like she's looking for something.

"There," she says, pointing straight ahead. "Right over there. See the break in the weeds? There's a dirt road."

I turn right onto the road as instructed, and all I can see is an old, ornate iron gate.

"Where are we?" I ask.

"Do you remember when I told you about the abandoned house my friends and I would go to in high school?"

"Yeah?" I see nothing but darkness.

"This is it."

"How do we get back there?"

"Climb the gate," she says, as if it was no big deal.

"Isn't this illegal?"

"Yes, but Nana knows the chief of police. It's fine."

My stomach is in knots as I park the car in front of the gate. I'm not sure if it's the spooky house or being alone with Micah that makes me so nervous. Maybe it's both.

Micah pulls two red electric lanterns from her backpack and turns them on before my headlights darken. I follow her to the fence and she hands both of them to me. She reaches a high bar on the gate and climbs over. She's clearly done this before.

"Oof," she says, wiping her hands on her jeans once her feet hit the ground. "I was afraid I'd gotten too fat to do that."

My heart drops. "Don't call yourself fat," I say.

She rolls her eyes. "Sorry," she says. "Force of habit."

Micah reaches through the gate and takes the lanterns from me. I also give her my keys, wallet, and phone before scaling the gate myself. I must say, she made this look a lot easier than it is. She has to talk me through it and tell me on which bars to place my hands and feet. When I'm safely on the ground on the other side, I breathe a sigh of relief before remembering I'll have to do it again when we leave.

"Don't worry," Micah says, as if reading my mind. "It'll be easier the second time."

I take a lantern and we walk down the long dirt driveway. I can vaguely make out a white house in the distance when the clouds finally part and the moon shines on the overgrown yard that was once a large homestead.

I gasp once it comes into view, then turn to Micah, who is absolutely beaming in the moonlight.

"It was built in the 1890s by a man in the lumber business," she says. "If we walked past the house, we'd see the river over the hill."

The home is gorgeous. It's a square Victorian, complete with belvedere and a wraparound porch. It has floor-length windows, though the glass has been broken in most of them. Someone spray-painted a picture of a marijuana leaf on the door and, between two of the windows, a picture of Snoopy with red eyes. But, despite the damage, I can still get a sense of the grandeur this property once conveyed.

"The graffiti wasn't us," Micah says. "That's new."

We walk up the stairs to the porch and let ourselves in through the broken window. Beer bottles and dirty clothes are scattered around the floor, but the home retains a lot of its original charm. The stairs have the original balusters, which are hand-carved with a magnolia design on each spindle. The house is a four-square layout with a single hallway running through the center. Cobwebs coat the chandelier in the foyer, which looks like it's missing a lot of its crystals.

At first I'm surprised the wallpaper isn't peeling off, then I realize it's not paper; the plaster was painted by hand. While I was disheartened by the graffiti outside when we arrived, I'm glad they spared the interior walls.

We walk through, room by room. Broken furniture is overturned and the rugs have been eaten away by time and rodents, but the floor seems solid. When we enter the back bedroom, I'm startled by my glowing, fractured reflection in a broken mirror above the fireplace in an elaborate frame as tall as I am. It looks to be original and was hung at an angle with the top a few inches away from the wall, allowing those on the floor to look up and see the full room. I haven't seen this in a house in a very long time, and I'm surprised it's still in place.

As we navigate the space, Micah tells me stories about her friends coming here with tarot cards and ouija boards, trying to summon the dead, when they were in high school.

"The only things we ever managed to summon were rats and the occasional opossum," she says, laughing.

All her stories involve Sistine, Patsy, and Kendall. It's a rare gift to have a core set of friends from grade school through decades of friendship. I can't help but feel a sense of envy. My high school was huge, and we all scattered after graduation. I run into some of them from time to time in the city, but we aren't close.

"Where is the kitchen?" I ask once we've made a complete circle around the first floor.

"Outside," she says, pointing out the window to a small outbuilding on the side of the house. "They updated the house with plumbing and electricity over the years, but never brought the kitchen to the main house."

We go upstairs, careful to avoid weak points in the tread. It's not as disheveled as the downstairs, probably because trespassers over the years were afraid they'd fall through the boards. I'm surprised by how many elements are unchanged despite the passage of over a hundred years.

The original tile and ironwork on the fireplaces are in excellent condition, and I recognize a stamp from a foundry that operated in Birmingham around the turn of the century.

We stop in one of the front bedrooms and I catch Micah looking out the window across the lawn. The moonlight catches her face and makes her skin glow like an angel. She looks like she belongs in this space, her old soul in a home that has witnessed more than a century of life. It just seems right.

"I always wished I could live here," she says, turning to me. "I'd have each room decorated in a different color and throw fabulous parties."

I imagine myself in that life with her. I couldn't ask for a better future for myself, or for us.

"It's a wonderful dream," I say. "Thank you for bringing me here. It's magical."

"You're welcome," she says. "I wish we could go up to the top. You can see all the way down the river from there, but last time I was here there were too many broken stairs."

"Who owns this place?"

"No clue. It's been abandoned since before I was born."

"That's a shame."

She looks heartbroken. "It really is. Places like this should be filled with love."

I put an arm around her. She leans into me and puts her head against my cheek for a moment before walking back downstairs. I follow her, careful to only step in spots where her feet have been.

Once we get downstairs, she turns in the foyer and

takes one last look around, but my eyes are glued to her. I step towards her, putting down my lantern and taking hers to rest it beside mine. I cup her face in my hands. Her big green eyes look up at me with a nervous intensity, and when our lips meet, I swear our feet come off the ground.

My skin is on fire.

As soon as Rhodes' lips touch mine, my entire being reacts. Time stops as we stand in the foyer of the old dilapidated house. His arms envelop my body and my heart is beating so hard I struggle to catch my breath. I never want this moment to end.

When he finally pulls away and looks at me, I lose it. I'm so completely overwhelmed with everything going on with Nana, with him, and with trying to figure out how to break things off with Garrett that the entire storm of emotions I've been trying to hold back all day bursts forth through my eyes.

Rhodes stands there and holds me, letting me lean all my weight onto him as I cry. I feel safe in his arms, and small, like he's shouldering the weight I've been carrying for what feels like an age.

I can't believe this is my life. I cannot believe a man like Rhodes is here, with me, in this house that has always been a refuge with the people I love. Despite Nana's illness and my world being tilted on its axis, I'm so happy to share this with him. So happy to finally feel safe and secure with a man. It's unreal. I've never had this.

He kisses me again, taking my face in his hands. Then he presses his lips to my forehead, my cheeks, the tip of my nose. I close my eyes and let the waves of desire pulse through me as I cling to him.

He steps back, looking at me through the shadows cast by our lanterns, which are both beginning to dimly flicker.

"We should go," he says. "Though I could stay here forever."

"Same," I say. Part of me wants to grab him and continue kissing him until the sun comes up, but if I let this go any further, I'm going to end up taking all my clothes off here and now. And while I love this house, it is filthy and I am not up to date on my tetanus shots.

We pick up our lanterns and make our way back outside. Bats circle overhead, flying out of the broken windows of the belvedere and into the night sky. Rhodes has his hand on the small of my back, his head down as we navigate the weeds.

We climb back over the fence and he has an easier go of it this time. Once we're back in the car, he leans over and kisses me again. It's all I can do not to pull my pants off and drag him into the back seat.

We're quiet on the drive home, but he reaches over the console and holds my hand. It's nice. No one has ever done that with me before.

When we get home, he walks me to the door.

"Do you want to come in?" I ask. I don't know if it's a good idea, but my body is screaming for him.

He sighs, running his hands through his hair, and bites his bottom lip.

"I want to," he said. "But I also want to make sure you're in the right headspace before we go any further. I know what'll happen if I go in. The last twenty-four hours has been a lot for you, and I don't want to take advantage of you when you're vulnerable."

Wow. Just wow. I didn't know a man could be this sensitive and empathetic.

"I understand," I say. "Thank you."

We kiss again—long, hard, and passionate—in the porch light. Crickets scream in the woods, and nearby, in the bushes, the whippoorwills sing their midnight song.

The next morning, I go straight to the hospital to check on Nana. She looks so much better. The color has returned to her face and she's more alert and chattier than she was the day before.

Yesterday I made the mistake of telling her about my plans with Rhodes. Now it's all she wants to talk about.

"Honey, I'm an old lady," she says. "Living vicariously through you is the most excitement I get."

I tell her about going to the old house on the river and exploring in the dark, but stop short of telling her about the kissing.

She knows better.

"And?" she asks.

"And nothing," I say, trying to end the details there.

"Micah, did he kiss you? Because if he didn't, I'm gonna call him myself and—"

"Nana! Don't call him! Yes, he kissed me."

"And?"

I roll my eyes. "That's where the details end."

She smirks. "You know, Pauline grew up in that house."

Of course she did. Knowing my luck, she'll probably haunt it when she dies.

Who am I kidding? Evil never dies.

"You never told me that," I say.

"Oh yeah! Her mama used to have these big, fabulous parties when we were young. I wasn't allowed to go, but I've heard the stories."

I smile, imagining the house coming to life despite the Pauline Cavendish connection. "I wish I could've seen it."

"I'm glad it went well with Rhodes," she says, changing the subject back to her favorite person. "I knew he was sweet on you from the moment he walked into the store. What are you going to do about that waste of time in Montgomery?"

I sigh and simply look at her. She raises her eyebrows and gives me an expression that says *Well?*

"I don't know, Nana. I'll probably break things off with him."

"Praise Jesus!"

"I'm glad you have your spirit back."

"Honey, if I'd died, I would've haunted you until you were done with that old rag."

I shake my head, then there's a knock at the door.

It's Rhodes holding a bouquet of roses. His hair is uncharacteristically disheveled and his expression is missing its normal stoicism, replaced by a shy twinkle in his eyes when he looks at me. My heart flutters.

"I'm on my way back to Birmingham," he says. "But I wanted to come check on you before I leave."

"Oh, you didn't have to do that," Nana says.

He sets the roses down on the table by the bed and leans in to give Nana a hug, which she gladly accepts. In fact, I don't think she'll ever let go of him. He tries to stand up a few times, but she's holding on for dear life.

"It's not every day I get a hug from a good-looking man," she says. "Humor me."

He laughs. "Yes ma'am."

She finally lets go. She asks about the work at the hotel, his family, and the upcoming jobs he has. He tells her they finalized plans for the Florablanca Inn, tells her about his son, and a few of the projects he's submitting bids on.

The latter makes me feel like crap. I've been so self-involved lately I haven't even asked him about his life. This is the first I've heard about any of these other buildings.

"I'm going to Memphis in a few days to look at a site," he tells her. "It's not as big of a project as the hotel here, but it is an old home that's being converted to a restaurant, so it should be fun. I'll know in a few weeks if I get the job."

"Oh, that sounds nice," says Nana. "You'll have to take Micah up there to see it." She winks at me and I smile, though I know I won't be going anywhere far away, since it would mean leaving her alone.

The nurse comes in to check on Nana and give her a bath, so Rhodes and I walk into the hall to give them privacy. Since it's lunchtime, he offers to take me to get something to eat, but I don't want to be away from Nana. He leaves instead to get me a sandwich at Bread Crumbs and brings it back, which only takes a few minutes.

He returns and we're eating in the lobby when Kendall, Patsy, and Sistine walk in. Even though it's late September, it's still warm enough for short sleeves, so Kendall is dressed in a flowy tank top, Patsy is wearing a 1950s housewife dress with lemons all over it, and Sistine is in her typical jeans, Converse, and vintage band t-shirt, today's choice being Pearl Jam.

I wave to them from my seat to get their attention, my mouth full of fried green tomato BLT. Rhodes stands when they walk over and gives them all hugs. They grin at me with the most excited looks on their faces.

"So things went well last night?" Patsy asks, clearly forgetting her filter.

"Yes, we hung out," I say, making a face for her to stop talking. She giggles.

"How's Nana?" asks Sistine.

"She's doing a lot better. They're giving her a bath."

We chitchat about some gossip Patsy heard at church that morning until the nurse comes out and tells us she's done. I shove the rest of my sandwich in my mouth and stand up. Rhodes takes my wrappers and throws them away.

"I need to get on the road," he says. "It was good to see you ladies again."

"You too," they all say, then give me grinning looks.

"We'll go ahead and go back," says Patsy, leading the other two down the hall to give us privacy.

"When are you coming back to Magnolia Row?" I ask.

"I don't know yet," he says. "As soon as I can. Hopefully, we will get all the permits and everything approved so we can get started soon. In the meantime, I'll probably be on the road a lot."

I look at him, disheartened. I don't want him to leave, but I know his life isn't here.

"I'd ask you to come see me," he says, "but I know with your nana—"

I shake my head. "I can't leave her," I say, "and she doesn't do well on long car rides, so I can't really bring her with me, either."

"I know," he says. "But I'll get back down here as soon as I can. Even if I have a few free days to spare, I'd rather be here with you than in my loft alone."

I hug him, and we kiss. His arms squeeze tight around my shoulders, and I ask him to text me when he gets home. He promises he will, then walks into the harsh mid-day light of the September sun.

leave the store closed Monday through Wednesday. Nana gets onto me for this, but it's simply too much to juggle. Besides, I'd rather be in the hospital with her during visiting hours. I miss Rhodes, but he texts throughout each day and calls every night before he goes to bed. He's quickly becoming my rock, and while it's scary to grow this attached to someone so quickly, I think I really need it right now. I can't imagine going through this alone. Each night, when I return home to the empty house, I want to cry. I don't even turn on the television. I just sit in the silence.

Nana is released on Wednesday, so I pick her up in my little blue hatchback. When the nurse wheels her out into the bright morning, she's holding the flowers from Rhodes in her lap.

"Who sent you roses?" the nurse asks, taking them from her and handing them to me so I can put them in the car. I buckle them into the backseat.

"Oh, a fine-looking young gentleman brought those to me," she says with the expression of a cat who just caught a canary. "I still got it."

The nurse laughs and tells her she'll miss her, but not to hurry back.

We get Nana secured in the car, then I take her home. Once she's comfortable in her recliner and watching Hallmark movies, I finally relax. I didn't realize how much stress I'd been carrying until things finally feel normal again. All at once, exhaustion and achiness hit me like a ton of bricks.

I leave Nana to her movies, light some candles in the bathroom, and take a bubble bath in the old pink tub. I nearly fall asleep listening to Lana del Rey, only waking up when my phone dings.

It's Garrett.

Hey gorgeous – you up for a visit this weekend?

I roll my eyes and put my phone down without responding. I'm not sure what to say to him. I don't want to see him this weekend. It doesn't feel right since I've now kissed Rhodes, though I'm technically not committed to either one of them. If I do break things off with Garrett, what do I even say? It's not breaking up if we're not together. What do I owe him, if anything?

I can't think about this right now. I don't want to think about anything, so I simply don't respond to Garrett for the rest of the night. By the time Rhodes calls for our nightly chat, I've completely forgotten about Garrett's text.

On Thursday and Friday, I leave Nana at home to rest while I go to the store. I take tons of pictures of the new stuff and schedule social media posts for the next three weeks, then continue Nana's job of cataloguing all the new items onto our spreadsheet.

I still haven't responded to Garrett, but before I'm

about to close up and go home to a quiet weekend, I get a text from him.

Hey sweetheart – did I do something? I'd really like to see you.

Sweetheart? That's new.

I ignore this text too.

After a trip to Piggly Wiggly to grab some things for dinner, I go home and start cooking. I watch a Lifetime movie with Nana, then get her settled in bed and wait for Rhodes to call while I read *Pride and Prejudice* for the hundredth time.

My phone rings, and instead of seeing Rhodes' name, I see Garrett's.

He never calls me. Like, ever. Not in the all the years we've been doing whatever it is we do.

I almost let it go to voicemail, then panic-answer at the last minute.

"Hello?"

"Micah! Hey."

"Is everything alright?"

"I…" he starts, his voice cracking. "I needed to hear your voice."

"You sound upset."

"There's a lot going on. Things at work are really bad right now. I'm afraid I'm gonna lose my company."

"I'm sorry," I say. "What happened?"

"Do you remember me telling you about the people we let go? They're suing for wrongful termination and other stuff. Now some of my current employees are making allegations. It's all total b.s., but my lawyer says I may have to pony up some funds I don't have. I'm … I don't know. I need a friend, and you're the only person I trust."

This catches me off guard. I'd gotten to a place where I thought I was done with Garrett, but hearing him so vulnerable and open for the first time tugs at me in a way I didn't expect. He needs me, and it feels good.

"That sounds awful," I say. "Is there anything I can do?"

"Can you come up tonight? I don't want to be alone. I'm not okay right now."

I pause to think. I don't want leave Nana, but she'll be going to bed soon. I know she's eaten and taken her meds, so she should be okay. And Montgomery isn't too far. It's not like driving to Birmingham.

"Micah, please?" he asks, his voice sounding weak and desperate.

"Only for an hour or two," I say. "My grandmother isn't doing well, so I don't want to be gone long."

"That's totally fine. Thank you, Micah. I miss you."

"Yeah," I say. "Me too."

*N*ana is tired, so I put her to bed and tell her I'm going out to meet friends. I put on a low-cut lavender shirt with long sleeves to hide my arms, thankful it's finally getting cooler outside and I can cover up without sweating to death. Rhodes calls on the drive, but instead of lying to him, I ignore the call completely.

When I get to Montgomery, I check my makeup in the

rearview mirror and head up to Garrett's apartment. He's in running shorts and a plain white t-shirt, and gives me a big hug when he sees me.

"God, I'm so happy you're here," he says. "It's been a shit week, and you're the only one I've wanted to talk to."

"Tell me what happened," I say.

We sit on his couch. I have to move a pile of dirty clothes and his video game controllers to clear a spot, but I figure he's been too stressed to worry about the state of his apartment. He relays a whole story about how some of his employees got together and decided they'd make more money from a lawsuit than actually working, so they purposely started performing poorly to bait him into firing them. He did, and they sued.

"There's some other money-grab schemes going on too, but I don't want to get into it. I guess when you're this successful, everyone wants to try to take it away. It sucks, because I worked so hard to build this company from the ground up all by myself. I don't deserve this."

The lines his face are tense and I can tell he hasn't been sleeping. I put my arm around him and he rubs my jeans-clad leg.

"It'll be okay," I say. "If you haven't done anything wrong, they won't win."

"What do you mean, *if* I haven't done anything wrong?" He's suddenly defensive and pulls away. "Of course I haven't."

"I didn't mean it that way," I say, taken aback by his combativeness. "I was only trying to say you have nothing to worry about. The truth will out, as they say."

"The truth will out? I've never heard that before in my life."

"It's from Shakespeare."

He shakes his head in a dismissive way. "I don't want to talk about this anymore," he says. "Let's go lay down."

We go to the bedroom and, for a little while at least, he's able to push his troubles aside and focus on being with me. It makes me happy to feel needed and wanted in a way I've never felt with him, and I feel closer to him now than ever before. I close my eyes and push away all my worries about Nana and the enormous guilt when I think of Rhodes.

I leave after a few hours. When I finally get home, Nana is snoring in bed and seems to be doing fine. I collapse in my room and my head spins. During the entire drive, all I could think about was how I've complicated everything with Rhodes. It makes me feel gross. I shouldn't have gone to Montgomery. It wasn't fair to Rhodes…or myself.

Reluctantly, I listen to a voicemail Rhodes left earlier. At the sound of his voice, I close my eyes and shake my head. He simply wanted to tell me to have a good night and he can't wait to see me again. I know we're not official, but it would hurt him to know what I've done tonight. I can't believe I've been so stupid.

I delete his voicemail, crawl under the covers, and close my eyes. When I dream, it's of Rhodes.

RHODES

The next few weeks fly by as I travel from Memphis to Louisville to Atlanta and Nashville. I even have a trip to New Orleans the week before Thanksgiving. Each of these projects is so unique and I'm absolutely loving getting to see these old buildings and dreaming about how we can bring each one back to life. It's exhilarating, not to mention validating every business decision I've made since I left my corporate job. Professionally, I'm having the time of my life.

Still, I miss Micah. This travel has taken me away from her, and I can't help but feel like she's slipping away. When we text, it takes her a while to reply. She usually answers when I call, but she seems distant and distracted. Part of me thinks she still may be seeing that other guy, which wouldn't technically be a betrayal since we haven't defined what it is we're doing. I really have no right to expect anything from her.

I just cannot stop thinking about our kiss. It was nuclear. That has to be a sign, right?

But what do I know? I've been out of the dating game for decades, and even before I was married, I had very little experience. This is all brand new for me.

I finally have a break while I'm waiting for responses to all the proposals I've sent out, so I decide to drive to Magnolia Row for the weekend. We're finally into October, so the heat isn't as oppressive as it was when I first started traveling there. In addition to seeing Micah, I'll finally get a chance to see the progress on the hotel. Jaxon found some great local contractors to work with and all our permits and plans were approved, so we're full speed ahead.

I call Micah the weekend before to see if she'll be able to see me.

"Oh!" she says when I tell her my plans. "Um, I may be able to. I'll have to see."

This really throws me off. She's all I have been able to think about since I left Magnolia Row. Did she not feel the fireworks when we kissed? Was all it in my head? Maybe I've already screwed things up before they even really got going. Maybe she finally realized I'm probably too old for her.

"If you have plans," I say, "don't feel obliged. I really enjoyed the last night we spent together. I thought you did too."

"I did," she says. Her voice is softer and I feel her guard come down a bit. "I do want to see you."

"So is that a yes?"

"Yes." This time I can hear the smile in her voice, and

my muscles relax. I didn't realize how tense I'd been until that point.

"Great! My schedule is pretty flexible, so let me know what works for you."

"Let's plan on Saturday night," she says, her voice finally sounding a bit lighter.

"Sounds good. I can't wait to see you, Micah."

"Same," she says, and we hang up.

I pour myself a glass of red wine, then cross my empty, sterile apartment and look out at the horizon of twinkling city lights. The city is bustling, Red Mountain is illuminated in the distance, and the streets below are crowded with people dining, drinking, and enjoying the beautiful night.

And all I want is to get in my car and drive straight to Micah.

MICAH

How have I gone from feeling like no man ever wants me to having two to choose from? It seems like a good problem to have, but it definitely is not.

On the one hand, Garrett has been super-sweet with everything going on at his work. I've been as supportive as possible, checking on him and making sure he's okay. We've only seen each other once since the night he told me about the lawsuits. He asked me for a loan to help with his legal expenses, so I took a few thousand out of savings to help him. I didn't tell anyone about it. Nana and my girlfriends would all have tried to talk me out of it, but it felt like the right thing to do. I'd like to think he'd do the same for me if I needed money.

Then there's Rhodes. Perfect, sweet, doesn't-need-me Rhodes, who is so far out of my league he may as well be on the moon. He's been nothing but upfront with me about how much he likes me, which is so overt it almost feels fake. Is it normal for guys to be so transparent, or is this a manipulation? There has to be a catch, because there always is. If only I could figure it out.

When Rhodes and I talk on Friday night about his plans to come to Magnolia Row the following week, I agree to see him despite my head spinning. I cannot juggle two guys. I'm not that girl. Granted, neither of them are my boyfriend, but it still doesn't feel right. It's not fair to them, and it's way too confusing for me.

I text my girlfriends, and Sistine agrees to meet me for a girl's night at Cattywampus the following evening. Patsy has too much going on with her five boys, and Kendall is in Florida visiting her parents.

I walk in, and our usual table is taken by a group of guys who look like they're twelve, but who in reality are probably well out of high school, so we sit at the bar.

Calista, the barkeep, knows us and brings our drinks without us having to tell her what we want. Since it's October, they finally have Dracula's Blood Orange on draft, so we each order one. Last year I raved about it so much that Calista suggested they rename it after me.

"How is Nana?" asks Sistine as we settle into our chairs.

"Slow," I say. "She's sleeping a lot and missing days at the store. And she doesn't talk much. I know she doesn't feel well."

"Sometimes it takes old people a long time to bounce back," she says. "I'm sure she'll be fine. She's a tough old broad."

I smile. "She is."

"Have you talked to Rhodes?" she asks.

"Almost every day," I say. "He's coming next weekend, which is why I wanted to talk to you. I need advice."

She raises her eyebrows, intrigued. "Please tell me you're going to sleep with him."

"What? No, that's not what I was going to ask."

She rolls her eyes. "From what you said about his kissing skills, I imagine he'll cure you of your attachment to the douchebag in Montgomery."

"Yeah. About Garrett—"

"Oh, here we go again. Micah, that guy is using you."

"He's not. He's sweet. And he needs me. Rhodes doesn't."

"Exactly. Rhodes chooses you with no ulterior motive. Better to be with someone who chooses you than someone who needs you for their own selfish gratification."

I sigh. She has a point. "Rhodes way too hot for me, Sissy. It makes me insecure." I surprise myself with the candor.

"First off, Rhodes is not too hot for you. From what I can tell, he's exactly what you need. But regardless of whether Rhodes is even in the picture, Garrett is bad for you. He's been that guy since you met, and he will always be that guy. You accept it because you don't think you deserve better, but you do. You always have. You're gorgeous, you're smart, and you have the biggest heart of anyone I know, which is what allows people to take advantage of you. It's beyond frustrating to watch."

I guess now would not be a good time to tell her about the money.

"Are you seriously still sleeping with Garrett?"

I bite my lip and hesitate. "Yes."

"How often?"

"Twice since Nana was in the hospital, but I didn't stay the night either time."

"Twice in one month? That's a record for him. He usually doesn't make much time for you."

"He's been struggling a lot, and it's made him open up more. I think we're getting closer."

Her interest piqued. "What is he struggling with?"

I close my eyes and take a deep breath. I tell her about the lawsuits and personnel issues his company is having, and she stares at me like she doesn't believe me. I do not mention the money. She would wring my neck, and I'm not ready to die.

"What is his last name again?"

"Bullingbrook. Why?"

"Just curious." She drinks her beer, never taking her eyes off me. "Look, Micah. He's not even here. He's never been here to see you. He's married to his work, as you've always said. You deserve someone who puts you first."

"You realize Rhodes is also not here and married to his work, right?"

"Rhodes is making a trip to see you, and he has further to go. Garrett has never been here. Ever."

"Well, it's hard for him to visit when I share a house with Nana. And Rhodes is mainly coming to see the hotel, not me."

"If Garrett really is some great successful business-man, he can afford a hotel room in Magnolia Row. There's no excuse." She's right again. "Give Rhodes a chance when he's here next weekend. That's all I'm saying."

We have a few more drinks and listen to a teenage girl with a guitar play an acoustic set of Taylor Swift covers. As we're leaving, Sistine stops me on the way to my car.

"Micah, if Rhodes and Garrett were here right now and you had to choose which one to go home with, who would it be?"

I pause.

"Don't think," she says. "Answer."

I stare into her eyes, and she knows my answer before I even have to say it.

"Rhodes."

The following Wednesday, I'm at work when Sistine texts me. She asks me if I can spare a few minutes to come meet her at her coffee shop. I check on Nana, who is in her office drinking unsweet—yes, I checked it—iced tea. It's her first day working this week and I can tell she's tired, but she needs to get out of the house. She gets depressed when she's cooped up.

"Go on," Nana says when I ask if she'll be okay for me to leave for a few minutes. "Tell the girls I said hello."

I drive to Bonny Beans, which is already closed for the day. Patsy and Kendall are there too, and Patsy unlocks it and lets me in. Sistine and Kendall are at a table covered in papers.

"Is this an intervention?" I ask.

"Kind of," says Kendall.

"Yes," says Sistine, shifting her weight in her chair. "It absolutely is. Sit down."

She pulls out a chair, then grabs a bottle of water for me.

"What is all of this?" I ask.

"Turns out no one can keep a secret from Patsy," says Kendall. "Even if you don't live in Magnolia Row."

"I did some digging on Garrett," Patsy says. "Which I should've done a long time ago."

I thumb through the piles of papers, which look like lawsuits. On the bottom are pictures printed from social media.

"I realize it's a lot," says Patsy. "But you really should know what's going on, which I doubt you do."

"Okay," I say, looking at them with apprehension.

"Garrett's company is in bankruptcy, and he's being charged with defrauding investors criminally and civilly. A ton of his female employees are suing him for sexual harassment. He also has a few restraining orders against him for stalking. The pictures in the back are from Vegas trips he's taken. It took me a lot of digging, but I managed to find them on other peoples' profiles."

My brain completely shuts down. I close my eyes and shake my head. "What?"

"Do us a favor and read through it," says Kendall.

"Your boy has a gambling problem," says Sistine, "not to mention a women problem, and I imagine an IRS problem at the rate he's going."

"Where did you even get these lawsuits?" I ask.

"My friend at church is a paralegal," says Patsy. "It's all on the state's website if you have access, which I now do."

"By the way," says Sistine, "the only thing she found on Rhodes is his divorce."

"Not even a speeding ticket," says Patsy.

I put my hands on the table, palms down, and stare at the mound of papers. How was I so stupid to think Garrett's kindness was genuine? Was he buttering me up because he needed money and attention? I can never tell them I gave him money. Never. This is humiliating. All I want to do is crawl under the table and cry.

"Thank you," I say, fighting back tears. "I mean it. I needed to see this."

"Take everything," says Sistine, handing me the papers. "We've already read it all."

I tuck the pile of evidence under my arm and stand up. "I have to get back to Nana," I say. "She's struggling a bit today."

"Send her our love," says Kendall. "And tell her my mama asked after her."

"I will."

I walk out, leaving my friends behind, and go back to the store. When I get there, Nana is leaning back in her chair, completely still. I freeze and stare at her for a moment, waiting for her to breathe. My ears pound in the overwhelming silence of the shop. After what feels like a full minute, but was probably only a few seconds, she lets out a huge snore, and it takes me a moment to catch my breath.

While she's sleeping, I rummage through the supply cabinet to find a big envelope and a blank piece of paper. I write *Don't call me again. -Micah* on the blank page and put it on top of the stack of lawsuits and pictures. I then write Garrett's address on the envelope, weigh it to calculate postage, and print the USPS label. It'll be in the mail tomorrow.

RHODES

The drive to Magnolia Row gets longer and longer each time I hit the road. It's over an hour of interstate, then miles and miles of farmland and forest. Even though it isn't cold, I see a dozen whitetail deer grazing on the side of the road, completely casual, like they aren't scaring every driver riding by.

For the whole drive, all I think about is Micah. I'm so eager to see her it feels like I'll never get there. I even skip through my Spotify playlist to find songs reminding me of her.

It's Friday, but she and I don't have plans until tomorrow night. She said she has a lot going on and needed to clear her head for a few days, but wasn't specific. I can only assume it's her grandmother, but I still have a sinking suspicion she may be dating someone else. At least she agreed to meet, though. That's promising. Surely she wouldn't let me drive all the way down here to see her just to say she wants to end things.

When I arrive in town, I go straight to the job site. Jaxon meets me there, along with Mrs. Caxton. It's a crisp fall day, probably the first hint of true fall this far into south Alabama, and she's dressed head-to-toe in leopard print spandex. I'm reminded of a Shania Twain video from the 90s where she wore a similar outfit. She's wearing black stiletto boots with the ensemble, and I'm not sure how she's going to navigate all this construction. It doesn't take long for me to realize the inappropriate footwear is her excuse to hold my hand while we walk around.

She's so absurd and so commanding of my attention it takes me a moment to even notice what's going on with the building itself. There are giant, bright blue tarps covering the entire roof. Massive jacks are in the crawlspace on the south wing of the hotel where we previously found rotten foundation. Piles and piles of wood are laying on that end, with a few more piles scattered across the property. There are two beams on the ground, one rotten and one that, while not brand new, is in excellent condition.

"I was able to salvage that piece from an old train station in Memphis," says Jaxon, pointing to it. "It was the right width and height already, but we had to cut it down to match the length."

The grounds of the property have also been cleared since I was last here, and while a good landscaper will need to be brought in to revitalize the exterior, it's easier to see how majestic this property was and will be again.

Jaxon has a copy of my plans, so we walk through as he shows Wilhelmina and me exactly what he plans to do in every square foot of the building, explaining how long everything should take. The whole property will need to be re-wired, a new roof put on, and the plaster walls will need to be replaced or patched in a lot of areas. I also let him know I found a vendor in Atlanta to restore the chandelier, and someone in Charlotte, NC, to work on the fountain for the lobby. My heart skips a beat every time I think of the fountain. For me, it will always be associated with Micah.

Wilhelmina is mostly quiet, which surprises me. She asks very few questions but occasionally will comment with a "marvelous" or "fantastic" and rub my arm in response to something Jaxon is saying. She winks at me often, and touches my back more than I'd like, but I remain stoic and pretend she's not flirting with me. A few times Jaxon gives me an amused look, which I also ignore.

Overall, I'm beyond pleased with how things are going. I have secured a few more jobs around the South from the proposals I sent out, but this one is particularly special. Wilhelmina's bottomless pit of money certainly helps. I've never not had a budget.

After we tour the property, we go to Southern Star Steakhouse for an early dinner. Wilhelmina drinks a lot of wine, is loud, and tells everyone she sees about her hotel, with an emphasis on the word "my" when she describes it. I don't see any locals I recognize, but they're all very kind and eager to hear all about the property. There's even a news reporter at the bar who gets our cards and tells us he's going to call for interviews next week. Wilhelmina is delighted. "Be sure to include my picture," she says with a huge smile. "I'll send you my media kit."

After we eat, I check into my hotel and text Micah. She says she's looking forward to seeing me, and we agree on dinner at Gator Tails for seafood the next night. I also ask about her grandmother, and she tells me Nana is tired but okay. She was able to go to the store one day that week, but it took a lot out of her, so she's been relaxing in her chair at home otherwise. I tell Micah I'm looking forward to seeing them both.

I spend the next day alone at the Florablanca Inn site, taking meticulous photos to document progress. Since it's Saturday, none of the construction workers are there, so it's easy to wander around and get lost in my own thoughts. In the distance, several boats pass by on the river, no doubt taking advantage of the mild weather, and frogs along the shore croak back and forth. It's an absolutely perfect, peaceful day, not to mention the best prelude to my evening with Micah.

I arrive at Micah's at exactly six o'clock. She meets me at the door wearing a low-cut, textured dark yellow dress with brown leggings and cowboy boots. The mustardy color makes her bright orange hair stand out, and she looks like the perfect picture of fall.

I give her a hug and kiss in the doorway, and I can see her grandmother watching us from the other room, beaming.

"Hello, Rhodes," she says in a flirtatious tone.

"Hello, Ms. Bonaventure," I say.

"Oh, call me Nana. Everyone else does. Or plain old Barbara."

"Yes ma'am."

"We're off, Nana," says Micah. "Do you need anything?"

"No, sugar bug. Y'all have fun."

"We will."

I open the door for Micah and show her to my car.

"She seems good," I say once we pull out of the driveway.

"She doesn't have any energy," she says. "We have an appointment with a cardiologist in Mobile in a few weeks, but I've been able to keep her blood sugar stable, so that's good."

"You do a great job taking care of her," I say. Again, I'm reminded of what a wonderful mother Micah would make and I feel guilty, but I push this thought away. She's assured me she doesn't want kids, and I have to take her word for it.

"Thank you," she says. "It's a lot, but I owe her."

"Does your mother know she was in the hospital?"

"I texted her, and she texted back a few times to check on things, but she didn't come or call. She has this way of doing the bare minimum so she doesn't feel like a completely horrible person."

"I'm sorry, Micah. That's a lot."

"It's okay." She takes my hand, and I feel a jolt of electricity run up my arm and straight to my heart. She has no idea how magnetic she is. My whole body reacts like I'm being struck by lightning when I'm around her.

The restaurant is off the beaten path; I doubt a GPS could even get me to it. We drive through the woods and into a clearing with a gravel parking lot and a building with a wraparound porch. Ceiling fans circle lazily in the autumn breeze coming off the river, and country music is blaring from the speakers.

Micah starts to get out but I touch her arm. "No," I said. "Wait here and let me get the door for you."

She looks at me, taken aback like she's never had a guy want to get her car door before. But she nods and waits as I walk around, taking her by the hand and helping her out of the SUV. Her boots crunch on the gravel, and her hand stays in mine as we walk into the restaurant. It feels good, like we're already a proper couple.

This restaurant houses more dead animals than a natural history museum. Taxidermy bass, marlin, snapper, and a few small alligators cover every wall. There are even several bucks with gigantic antlers. Each has a plaque underneath with the name of the hunter or fisherman and the date of kill/catch. Some of them even have names, like a bass named "Leroy Brown" behind our corner table by the window.

Micah sees me staring and chuckles.

"I guess it's a lot if you aren't used to it, huh?"

"Well, their branding is effective," I say.

"The food is great. I hope you like seafood. The catfish is caught locally, but everything else is brought up from the Gulf each day."

"Sounds delicious!"

The waitress brings a huge bowl of hushpuppies. The

outside looks burnt, but the inside is perfectly moist, with tons of onions and not too much grease.

"These are amazing," I say to Micah as she pops one in her mouth, somehow not smudging her red lipstick.

"I could eat these every day," she says.

We look over the menu, and I order the shrimp and grits and Micah gets crab cakes with asparagus. We also each get a Cattywampus beer.

Once the waitress leaves, Micah's face gets serious.

"Listen, Rhodes," she begins with a dark tone. My stomach drops. I hope this isn't the we-should-be-friends conversation. "I owe you an apology."

I'm confused. "For what?" I ask.

"To be honest, I was kind of dating someone. I mean, not officially, but I was talking to someone for a long time when I met you. I may have mentioned it before but I should've been more upfront about it, since I know you like me. If I seemed like I was distant or being weird, that's why."

I note her use of past tense verbs. "You aren't seeing this person anymore?"

"No," she says. "Turns out, he wasn't such a nice guy. He wasn't with me for the right reasons."

I nod, pause, and decide to put all my cards on the table. "Are you telling me this because you're interested in being with me?"

"Maybe," she says. "I do like you. But, to be honest, I'm kind of afraid. I mean, we live in different cities, which was one of the challenges with the other guy. It was easy for him to hide things from me and keep me at a distance. I also…" She looks down and fidgets with her nails.

"What?" I ask, reaching out to her. She puts her hands in mine.

"I still don't know why you like me."

"Micah, we've been over this. You're far too good for me. My concern is I'm too old for you. If you like me and we want to give this a chance, you'll be giving up being a mother. I'm too old to start over with a baby. I don't want you to get to a certain age and begin to resent me for it."

"That's the least of my concerns right now. I told you I don't want to have kids anyway."

I nod. I know she has a lot going on with her grandmother, but I also know once her grandmother is no longer here, when Micah is alone with no one to care for, she may want to fill the void with a new family. I don't say this out loud. The last thing I want to do is upset her.

"As far as the distance goes," I say, "if we're both committed and decide this is what we want, we'll figure it out. Before we start making promises, I'd like to get to know each other better, if you're open to it."

She nods. "I am," she says. "You'll have to be patient with me. I need baby steps. I'm not good at this. And, to be honest, I'm absolutely terrified."

I take a deep breath. "I can do that."

Our beers arrive and we spend the rest of the evening drinking, eating, and talking about all the jobs I've been hired to work on, antiques she's sold to different people around the state, and a completely ridiculous romance novel she's reading about alien vampires.

"It's not the kind of thing I normally pick up," she says, "but it sounded so absurd I couldn't resist."

Her cheeks are rosy from laughing. I love how light-hearted she is, despite her tone when this date started. Even with everything going on, she has this ability to capture and enjoy those little moments of bliss most people don't take time to see. It's refreshing.

At the end of the night, I walk her to my car. My cheeks hurt from smiling and all I want to do is take her back to my hotel, but I also don't want to be *that* guy.

"Where next?" I ask, putting the ball in her court.

She hesitates, looks at me in the blue glow of my dashboard lights, and bites her bottom lip. She does this a lot when she's thinking.

"I want to say *your hotel*," she says. "But I also want to take things slow, so let's go back to my house. I know I'll keep my clothes on if we stay there."

I nod, then start the car. "We could always go back to our house on the bluff," I say.

"Our house," she says. "I like that. Even if it crumbles and falls into the river, it will always be our house."

"It will." I take her hand and kiss it. She looks at me with a closed-lip smile and my heart melts. She's my soulmate. I know it in my bones.

I start the car and drive back to the home she shares with her grandmother. The outside lights are on, but the inside is dark.

"You can come in if you want," she says. "Just for a little while."

I nod, and we go inside. She checks on her grandmother, who is snoring in her room.

She fixes each of us a glass of wine and we sit on the couch. The room is dimly lit by two Tiffany lamps, which cast a delicate glow on Micah's pale skin.

We barely drink any of the wine. Instead, we spend the next few hours holding each other, our lips locked and hands wandering.

MICAH

The rest of the year flies by in a fog. Nana continues to deteriorate, and I go through the motions of the holidays, knowing it'll probably be my last year to enjoy these times with her. The doctor we see in Mobile says her heart disease has progressed, and though I've done a good job monitoring her blood sugar, I still catch her sneaking candy or sugar in her tea from time to time. It's like she's given up and doesn't care anymore. It's hard not to take that personally.

My mother continues to send the occasional text, but spends Thanksgiving and Christmas with her new boyfriend and his kids. I know it sounds bad, but I'm glad she's not here. She brings drama, and that's the last thing my nana needs, even though I know she misses her daughter. It's a no-win situation, and I hate it for her.

Rhodes spends Thanksgiving and Christmas in Birmingham with his son and is only able to visit Magnolia Row about once a month, which confirms my suspicion that this long-distance thing isn't going to work. We haven't slept together yet, for two reasons. First, I had to get myself checked out after I found out about all the shenanigans Garrett had been up to. Even though he and I had always used protection, I was paranoid and wanted to make sure I was clean.

I am. Thank God.

Even after all the tests came back negative, I'm still stalling with Rhodes, and I make a million excuses. I hate to admit it, but the truth is I'm terrified of him seeing me naked. I'm dumpy little small-town nobody. He's Mr. Rockstar Architect touring the South and saving all these buildings from certain death. When I look in the mirror, I see a big girl. When I look at him, I see a man oozing confidence and quiet sex appeal.

I am way too insecure to make this relationship work. I will never feel good enough. Ever. I do miss him, but I don't want to make any demands if I'm not ready to commit. And I'm not.

I don't know if I ever will be.

New Year's Eve is hard, and I've been dreading it. Nana hasn't been feeling well all day, so I tell Sistine I'm busy and can't go to the big midnight bash at Cattywampus.

Rhodes calls from a hotel in Nashville. He's there for the wedding of a former colleague, and though he invited me to come with him as his date, I couldn't leave Nana. The entire day I spend thinking about all the beautiful, skinnier women in their skin-tight designer dresses flirting with him and dancing and making him realize he actually can do better.

My head spins all night. I'm sick with jealousy over women I've completely invented in my own head. It's exhausting.

Nana goes to bed early. I tuck her in and she's out before I can even turn off her light. I have a bottle of rosé in the fridge, so I open it and drink the entire thing while flipping through the channels showing cheesy NYE party specials. Rhodes sends me texts throughout the night, checking on me, and even sends me a selfie he took in the hotel mirror before he left for the wedding. He's wearing a sharp navy pinstripe suit tailored perfectly to his tall, lean body. It takes my breath away when I see how sexy he is, how masculine and classy, like Mr. Darcy without the grumpy exterior. I wish more than anything to be with him tonight.

At midnight we do a video call. He's still at the wedding, and I can tell there's a huge party going on behind him. We have a fake toast with our respective glasses, and blow kisses to each other. I tell him I miss him, then we hang up.

I slide off the couch in my lime green silk pajamas, wash my wine glass, and get ready for bed while I listen to Taylor Swift. I turn it off when I walk down the hall to my bedroom.

I pause at my door, which is right beside Nana's. I listen

for the sound of her soft snoring, but don't hear anything. I close my eyes, hold my breath, and wait.

And wait.

A pit of dread forms in my stomach as I crack open her door. She hasn't moved. I tiptoe to her bedside and put my hand on her chest above the covers. Nothing. I turn on the lamp beside her bed. She's paler than normal, and when I touch her hand, it's cold.

I sink to the floor. She's gone—I know it without even calling an ambulance. The room spins and a weight falls on my chest, making it hard to breathe. I look at her again. She's so peaceful, her white hair spread out on her pillow like an angel.

This cannot be happening. I know no life without my nana. I can't function without her. I don't even know what to do in this moment without her to tell me how to handle it. My brain is firing off in so many directions I'm frozen in place.

I don't know how long I sit on the floor. An endless stream of tears rolls down my face, but I'm not sobbing. I'm in shock, though I shouldn't be. This has been a long time coming, but I didn't want to believe it could really happen. How can she be taken from me?

I've never felt so alone in my life.

I take my phone from the pocket of my pajama pants. My hands are shaking so badly I drop it twice before I'm able to call 911. The operator is a girl I went to high school with, so I don't even have to give her the address. While I wait for the ambulance, I sit on the side of the bed with Nana, stroking her hair and focusing on my breathing.

Should I call Rhodes? My friends? My mom? The funeral home? I'm not prepared for this. I simply don't know what motions to go through or how to process. Nana always took care of everything. She knew what to do, no matter the situation.

I don't even know where to begin.

Once the coroner and paramedics arrive, I sit alone in the living room while they tend to Nana in the bedroom. I'm on the edge of the sofa, arms wrapped around my stomach and rocking back and forth while people hurry past. The coroner, who also runs the only funeral home in Magnolia Row, stops to extend his condolences and asks me to call him the next day to go over arrangements. I nod with a jerky, stiff neck, still in shock. He asks me if he can call anyone for me, but I say no. I don't even know why I say no. It pops out of my mouth like someone else is saying it.

When they take her out of the house, I turn my head and close my eyes. I can't see a lumpy white sheet and know the most important person in my life is leaving this house for good. It's too much to wrap my head around, an image I don't want burned into my memory.

Everyone who came to help is incredibly kind, but once Nana is in the ambulance, they say goodbye.

And I am left with silence.

My ears ring from the eerie quiet in the house. Suddenly my chest feels heavy and I'm struggling to breathe. The dam breaks and I begin sobbing so hard I sink to my knees and curl up on the carpet. All the anxiety I'd felt throughout Nana's illness, her hospitalization, and everything catches up with me in a rush of uncontrollable tears. When I finally catch my breath, I look around the house and tremble. This is my new reality.

I'm completely and utterly alone.

I look at my phone. I should call one of my girlfriends to come over. I know any of them would get out of bed in a heartbeat to be with me, but all I want is Rhodes. Even though he's six hours away in Nashville, I dial his number.

RHODES

I'm asleep in my hotel room on Broadway when my phone rings. I only half-acknowledge it, part of me thinking the buzzing is a dream.

When it doesn't stop, I rub my eyes and look at the screen, which is blurry without my contacts. The sound of laughter and drunken voices from the nearby country bars echoes below my window as I stare at Micah's picture illuminated in the darkness. It's three in the morning. Something must be wrong.

"Hello?" I answer, my voice tired. All I hear on the other end are sobs. Micah's sobs.

My heart drops. I know what this means.

The last few times I've been to Magnolia Row, her grandmother had been looking more and more frail. I was afraid she wasn't long for this world. That's the only explanation for the hysterical cries I'm hearing on the other end of the line.

"Micah," I say, as soft and smooth as I can. "Micah, it's okay. I'm here." She keeps crying. I repeat, over and over, "It's okay. You're okay. Just breathe."

When her breath stabilizes, she finally speaks. "I'm sorry to call you so late," she says with a shaky voice. "I don't know what to do."

"I know, sweetie. Calm down. We'll figure it out."

She sighs hard. "I think I'm in shock," she says.

"It's okay. That's normal."

"They took her away, and I'm sitting here alone. You're the only person I could think of to call."

I sit up in bed. "I'll be there as soon as I can," I say. "You don't have to go through this alone."

This makes her start crying hard again, and I simply hold the phone and listen to her until she's ready to talk. God, I wish I hadn't gone to this stupid wedding. I should've known something like this would happen, and now I'm six hours away.

"I'll be fine until tomorrow," she says. "I'm sorry I bothered you in the middle of the night."

"It is tomorrow," I say. "And it's no bother at all. I'm glad I'm the first person you called. If I leave Nashville now, I can be there by ten in the morning. I'll help you with everything. I went through this when my mom passed."

"Thank you, Rhodes. I…" She hesitates, her voice panicked and cracked. "I'm so lost."

"I know. But I'll hold your hand through everything. We'll get through it together. In the meantime, call Sistine or Patsy if you need anything before I get there."

"I will. I may wait until the sun comes up, at least."

"Okay. I'll be there as soon as I can."

"Thank you," she says. "Bye, Rhodes."

"Bye, Micah."

Without so much as yawning, I roll out of bed, take a quick shower to wake myself, throw my things in my bag, and check out as quickly as I can. When I get to my SUV, I tell the GPS to take me to Magnolia Row, and I'm on the road before the sun rises.

After a quick stop in Birmingham to pick up some extra clothes, I make my way to south Alabama. When I pull up to Micah's house, there are several cars in the driveway. I park and walk to the patio door, where I can see Sistine and Patsy talking in the living room. They wave me in as soon as I get there.

"She's on the phone with her mother," Sistine whispers, pointing to Micah, who is sitting at the dining room table, back to us, with her hand over her face and her phone to her ear.

We stand in silence and wait, trying to make out what she's saying. Finally, she puts the phone down and rubs her face.

I step into the dining room and put my hand on her shoulder. When she turns to look at me, a flood of relief comes over her and she stands to hug me. I squeeze her as tight as I can, and she leans on me while she quietly cries into my shirt.

"I'm sorry you had to drive all this way," she says.

"It's okay," I say. "There's nowhere else I'd rather be."

I release my hug and kiss her on the forehead. She looks up to me with swollen eyes.

"My mother is coming," she says, her voice low and full of dread.

"And cue the drama," says Sistine, who is standing in the doorway.

"That's alright, girl," says Patsy. "You got a tribe behind you."

Micah nods and leans into my shoulder. Patsy's right. Even without blood relatives, she still has people who love and care about her. She has the family she chose, the ones who continue to choose her.

That day, we go through the motions of meeting with the funeral director and the pastor from the church. It turns out Ms. Barbara planned and paid for everything long before she died, right down to the flowers and hymns she wanted. All Micah has to do is get a copy of the contract to make sure she doesn't want to add anything.

The house is incredibly busy. Everyone in town wants to stop by with casseroles and flowers. I probably meet half of Magnolia Row in the span of eight hours, and each time someone asks if I'm Micah's boyfriend, I laugh awkwardly and say we're getting to know each other. Honestly, I'm not sure what else to say. We haven't exactly defined anything, and now is not the time for me to force the issue.

I offer to stay at the local hotel to give Micah space, but she insists I not leave her, so I don't. I put my things in the guest room, but for the next two nights I sleep with her in her bed, though the physical contact never goes beyond kissing. She's not ready to go further.

The morning of the funeral arrives and Micah hasn't slept at all. The rising sun casts a soft orange hue on the curtains as we're laying in bed, talking. The house is as quiet as a church, so I'm startled and sit straight up when I hear the side door open and keys clang on the kitchen counter.

"Oh God," Micah says, her eyes closed. "She's here."

I know she means her mother without even asking. She gets up and tiptoes out the door. She's still in her floral pajama pants and a hoodie from Victoria's Secret. I follow, wearing my comfy pants and an Auburn University College of Architecture t-shirt.

Piles of bags dot the living room floor, and I can tell from Micah's expression she's already annoyed. The side door is open, and her mother is dragging in more stuff to dump in the living room amongst the dozens of plants and flowers Micah has received in the past few days.

If I didn't already know who she was, I never would peg her as Micah's mom. She's short where Micah is tall. She's very skinny, lacking all the curves Micah has, and has chin-length, straight dark hair. The shape of their noses and eyes are the same, but that's where the similarities end. Her chaotic energy makes me anxious, and I can tell Micah too is frazzled.

"Mother," she says. "You're here."

"Micah." Her mom puts a hand on her hip and gives Micah a once-over. "You look like hell."

Micah shakes her head and rolls her eyes.

"Come on, give me a hug," the mother says, reaching out. She grabs her and squeezes, though Micah barely reciprocates the gesture. "Who are you?" the mom says, looking at me.

"I'm Rhodes," I say.

"Christa Bonaventure," she says, eyeing me with suspicion.

"Mom, this is my, um, my friend. Rhodes Cauley." Apparently I'm not the only one who struggles to define our relationship.

"By the looks of it, he's more than a friend."

"That's really none of your business," says Micah. "Besides, don't you have your own new relationship to worry about?"

"It's kind of a wait and see thing."

"I thought you were living together and playing stepmom to his kids."

Her mother shrugs and offers no further explanation.

I look at the mounds of stuff and it suddenly hits me— she did not pack for a short trip. I peer out the window to her small car, and it's full to the brim. She has no intention of leaving.

Micah seems to have this realization the same time I do. She shakes her head.

"I can't deal with this right now," she says, walking to her bedroom. I turn to follow her.

We close the door, and in the background we hear bustling and bumping as her mom moves more stuff into the house.

"She seriously can't be moving in," Micah says.

"It looks like she intends to," I say. "Micah, all you need to do is get through today. You can worry about that later."

I want to ask if her grandmother had a will, or if there were any talks about what happens to her home and the store when she passed. I wonder whose name is on the deeds, and if her mom has access to bank accounts that should, in all fairness, go to Micah. But now is not the time, so I table that conversation.

I just hope Ms. Barbara foresaw this happening. Surely she knew her own daughter.

I go to the kitchen to get a bottle of water and to give Micah some privacy while she gets ready for the funeral. The visitation starts at ten, followed by a graveside service and lunch at the local Presbyterian Church. Before visitation, Sistine suggested we come to Bonny Beans for coffee and breakfast, so that's our plan. Patsy and Kendall are also supposed to meet us there.

Her mother says nothing to me as I watch her drag bag after bag back to Micah's grandmother's bedroom. My heart sinks. It's not my place to say anything, but I know this will upset Micah.

I look out the back window. As I drink my water, two

deer, a doe and a faun, wander through the back yard. The sun casts a hazy yellow glow over the dead winter grass and a cold breeze rustles the brittle leaves in the magnolia tree at the back of the yard. Despite the tension in the house, the world outside is at peace.

Once I finish my water, I proceed down the hall and find the bathroom door open, where Micah is finishing her make-up. Her hair is curled and her face is flawless despite her puffy eyes. She's wearing a black sweater dress with white trim, leggings, and boots. Her bright red lipstick pops against the dark colors. For a woman in mourning, she's a vision.

She catches me watching. "Patsy brought me water-proof mascara," she says. "I'll need it today."

Her mom walks to the bathroom in a huff and asks how much longer she'll be.

"I don't know," Micah says, her voice curt and flat.

I know Micah has told me time and time again about her mother, but this coldness and complete disregard for empathy is so much worse than I'd imagined.

Her mother walks back to Ms. Barbara's bedroom and closes the door.

"Is she moving into Nana's room?" Micah asks.

"I think so," I say, studying her face for a reaction.

She looks sad, shaking her head and turning her attention to her eye makeup. She puts the final touches on her lashes, gives me a hug, then tells me to hop in the shower before her mother can take the bathroom. She goes to the guest room and fetches my toiletry bag and clothes while I fiddle with the water temperature.

"I can't tell you how much it means to me for you to be here," she says.

I nod. "I know, Micah."

She smiles, gives me a kiss, then leaves me alone to undress and shower.

When I emerge from the bathroom, I'm dressed and ready to go. Micah is in the living room staring out the window, her face completely blank. When she realizes I'm there, she stands and grabs her purse.

"We're leaving!" she calls down the hall to her mother, who pops her head out of the bedroom.

"So the bathroom is free?"

Micah rolls her eyes and says nothing.

Heavy footsteps plod down the hallway. For a tiny woman, Micah's mother is loud.

"I thought the visitation started at ten," she says, poking her head into the living room. She's wearing nothing but a bra and shorts, and I turn my eyes so she doesn't think I'm trying to stare.

"We're meeting my friends for breakfast."

There's an awkward pause. "Nice dress," her mom says, as if surprised. "That's a good cut for a big girl."

I glance at Micah and she looks down, embarrassed.

"You can't—" I begin, ready to admonish this woman for talking like that to her daughter, but Micah cuts me off.

"It's not worth it," she whispers to me. "Goodbye, Mother," she says.

And with that, we turn to leave.

On the drive to the coffee shop, I tell Micah several times how beautiful she is, but she shakes her head and puts her hand up as if telling me to stop talking, so I do. I know her mom got under her skin, and there's nothing I can do or say to make it okay.

I wish I could make this entire nightmare disappear for her. It's beyond difficult to watch.

MICAH

Just get through the day.

Get through the day, and tomorrow I can deal with whatever shit my mother dragged in. I can figure things out with Rhodes, and I can try to find my new normal.

All I need is to get through this day. One heavy step at a time.

At least my dress is a "good cut for a big girl." I roll my eyes every time those words echo in my brain. It's not surprising, coming from my mother, but I wish she hadn't said them in front of Rhodes. I already feel like we're mismatched somehow without anyone bringing it to his attention.

We hardly talk on the way to the coffee shop. I want to forget everything from this morning and focus on saying goodbye to my nana. While Rhodes drives, I close my eyes and focus on my breathing, hoping this will calm me enough to not fall apart.

When we arrive, Sistine has a table reserved for us in the back corner, and Patsy and Kendall are waiting.

"Oh, honey, you look beautiful," says Patsy, giving me a big hug.

"You do," says Kendall, who also squeezes me.

They each give Rhodes a hug in turn, and we sit as Sistine approaches with tea, coffee, and bagels. Once we're fed, Sistine sits with us and I proceed to tell them about my mother arriving with her chaos.

"She can't stay there," says Sistine. "That should be your house."

"Surely Nana had a will," says Kendall. "She planned for everything else."

I shake my head. "I can't think about any of that right now. I'll deal with it later."

"Of course," says Patsy. "But if we need to go over there and kick her out, you let me know. I'll throw her in the back of Garion's truck and haul her you-know-what out of town. Maybe we can feed her to Kendall's alligator."

This gives us the laugh we very much need, and we spend the rest of breakfast talking about the chilly but cooperative weather, how many people we expect to see at the service, and Kendall's movie star boyfriend coming back to town. By the time we leave, I'm feeling more relaxed and at peace with what I have to do.

The visitation, the service, and lunch go by in a fog. Most of Magnolia Row turns up, and Patsy has to stand beside me and remind me of who some people are. Rhodes stands at a polite distance throughout, checking on me frequently and calming me simply by being there.

Every time I look up to see him across the room, I feel stronger.

My mother, on the other hand, is all over the place. She goes from crying with Nana's friends to laughing with people from her high school class. She sees this as The Christa Show, and I struggle to not show my annoyance.

"Ignore her," Sistine whispers several times under her breath.

Apart from my mother, the day is nice. Everyone has lovely things to say about Nana, and even Pauline Cavendish, dressed head-to-toe in black sequins and wearing a giant hat with a fake crow glued to the top, shows up at the visitation to pay respects. For the first time in my life, I appreciate her "airing out her crazy," as Nana always said. She looks completely absurd, but it makes me laugh, which I need.

"Your grandmama was the only woman in town worth a damn," Pauline says to me before giving my mother a dirty look. "Good luck with that one," she adds, nodding towards my mom, who is telling a story to someone I don't recognize and waving her hands around like a drama queen.

With that, Pauline walks to the back and says something to Rhodes. He blushes, then looks at me as she leaves. I wonder what she said, but I don't have time to think too much about it before the next person in line is waiting to give me a hug.

When we're finally alone in the car once it's all over, I ask Rhodes about it.

"She said I'm an idiot if I don't snatch you up," he says.

"I know she's a lunatic, but I think she really loved your nana."

"Everyone did," I say, then quietly cry as he drives me home.

Dozens of people show up at home with more food and more flowers. Patsy even has to pus some of the casseroles her car to put in her freezer since I ran out of room.

By evening, everyone clears out save Rhodes and my mother. Patsy has to get home to her kids, Kendall's boyfriend is leaving tomorrow to go back to LA, and Sistine has to go to the coffee shop to make sure her employees cleaned and closed the store properly.

"Well," my mom says, "I told a guy I went to high school with I'd meet him up at Cattywampus for some drinks."

I'm sitting on the couch next to Rhodes when she says this. We're holding hands and I'm leaning on him.

"How long are you staying?" I ask, knowing full well this is a loaded question.

My mom cocks her head to the side and looks like she's bewildered I'd ask.

"Well, this is my house now," she says.

My heart sinks. I do not want to deal with this.

"Nana left you the house?" I ask.

"I'm her only daughter. Of course she did."

"Did she have a will?" I'm struggling to hide the contempt in my voice.

My mom storms out of the room and comes back with a document that looks like it was signed by Nana. It's short, barely two pages. Rhodes and I read through it, and it says all her property and assets are to go to my mother. Rhodes says nothing, but gives me a concerned look.

"We'll talk about the store and everything later," she says. "I gotta go." She grabs her jacket and purse and walks out the door.

My stomach turns and my face gets hot. "I feel sick," I say to Rhodes.

"Micah, we can talk to a lawyer. This doesn't look like a properly probated will and—"

I hold up my hand to stop him from talking.

"My brain can only process so much at a time, and I'm way beyond my bandwidth for the day," I say. "Maybe for the month."

"I understand," he says.

I shake my head. "I can't stay here with her," I say.

"We can get a room at the hotel."

I nod and get up to pack my bags while Rhodes also collects his things. My entire body feels heavy as I grab my clothes, a few books, and my favorite pink blanket.

Rhodes meets me in the living room, takes my bags, and loads them in his car. I stand in my living room, looking around in disbelief. The only life I've ever known is over. The person most important to me in the world is gone. My home is gone. My store and my career are probably gone too.

How do people get through this? It's physically painful. Every fiber of my being is heavy and screaming "no." The simple act of walking feels like dragging lead.

"I hate to say this," Rhodes says, coming back into the house. "But if there's anything of your grandmother's of any value, sentimental or otherwise, you may want to take it with you."

He has a point. I walk back to her room, stepping over the mounds of bags and loose clothes my mother left scattered all over the place. I grab a Piggly Wiggly tote full of my mother's shoes, dump it in the floor, and place Nana's jewelry box inside. I also grab some photos, a Wedgwood ring tray, and Waterford crystal cross she bought on a trip to Ireland with my grandfather. I also take the orange and brown crocheted afghan off the bed and hold it to my face. It still smells like Nana, and it's all I can do to keep from sobbing.

Rhodes leads me to the car, his hand on my back. I take one last look at the house as he drives me to the hotel.

I cancel my site visits and teleconferences for the next week as I figure out how best to support Micah. She's completely shut down. We only stay in the hotel in Magnolia Row for one night. When she wakes up the next morning, she tells me she wants to completely get out of town, at least for a while.

So, I drive her to Birmingham. When we get to my condo, she crashes on the bed, despite the fact that it's only lunchtime, and doesn't get up until evening. I have pizza delivered, and once we eat, she goes straight back to sleep.

The next few days go by exactly like this. She wanders around like a zombie, occasionally showers, and only eats when I put food in front of her.

After a week, I finally convince her to go to dinner with me at Chez Fonfon though I know she doesn't want to. Even so, she showers, does her makeup, and wears a gorgeous green sweater dress that hugs her curves and makes her emerald eyes look like something out of a dream. Once she's ready, I can see a hint of her sparkle coming back.

At dinner she seems lighter, and I can tell getting out of the condo is good for her. Her face glows in the low light and there are moments when she forgets about everything in Magnolia Row. It's just the two of us, having dinner like it's something we do all the time—together, as a proper couple. It feels right. I know her heart isn't here, but I don't ever want her to leave.

The next day we go for a long walk at the Birmingham Botanical Gardens, then wander around the art museum, where she finally gets to see the massive collection of Wedgwood pottery I've been telling her about since we met. Her face lights up when she sees it, and she talks about how much her grandmother would've loved it. It's the first time she's talked about Nana without crying.

Finally, after she's been in my condo for two weeks, I'm sitting at the drafting table in my office working on some blueprints for the project in Memphis when Micah walks in from the bedroom.

"Rhodes," she says. "We need to figure out what we're doing."

I turn to her, relieved. I've been wanting to have this conversation, but was too afraid to broach the subject—afraid it was too soon after her nana died, afraid she would say she wants to be alone, afraid she wants to start a new family now that she doesn't have anyone to take care of.

"I agree," I say.

"I don't know how I would be getting through this time

without you," she says. "And I lack the vocabulary to explain how deeply I love you right now."

I'm taken aback. "I love you too, Micah," I say.

"I don't know what our future looks like, or if we even have future," she says. "You have a beautiful place here, and a career, and all the excitement a big city like this can offer. I'm a small town girl. While it is nice here, I can't imagine making a life in this city, even with you. My home is in Magnolia Row. My friends are in Magnolia Row. My store, if it even is mine anymore, is in Magnolia Row."

I take a deep breath. "I don't want you to give up anything for me," I say. "When you think about your life at home, does it include me? Or are you wanting a fresh start with someone younger? Someone who can give you a family?"

"Could my life in Magnolia Row include you?" she asks.

"I can do my job from anywhere. If you want to be with me, we will make it work. But I want to make sure you're serious before we go any further. Fifteen years is a big age gap, and I feel like you'll be giving up a lot to be with me."

"If you're talking about the kids thing, I already told you it's not an issue," Micah says. "This week, I've been thinking a lot about my life up to this point. My entire adulthood has revolved around taking care of my nana. I don't regret a minute of it, and I'd continue to do it every day if it meant keeping her forever, but now that chapter is over. I want to take care of me. Focus on me. I see what Patsy goes through with her boys, and God bless her for it, but it looks exhausting."

"To be fair," I say, "she does have five kids. One is easier."

Micah laughs. "True. Even so, this next chapter in my life needs to be about freedom. I want to go to museums, travel, grow my antique business, have drinks with my friends without worrying about someone at home who needs me to pack their lunch or wipe their butt." She sighs and closes her eyes. "I have a lot to figure out in terms of where I'm going to live, how I'm going to get my store back and all of that, but this week here with you has been enlightening. A breath of fresh air, truly. It's been good for me to get out of Magnolia Row and get some perspective. But now I'm ready to go back. And I hope you'll go with me."

"Absolutely."

"So are we official?"

"We are."

She walks across the room and we kiss, long and passionately. We've spent night after night sleeping together in our clothes, cuddly and chaste, but finally her walls come down and her hands are all over me. My body is on fire as she touches me under my clothes, and it's all I can do to get her to the bedroom before we completely lose ourselves.

MICAH

Last night with Rhodes was the most amazing experience I've ever had with a man. Not only did he know exactly what he was doing, but I finally felt comfortable enough to let him see me. All of me. No leaving the bra on, no covering my stomach, no turning the lights off so he doesn't see my cellulite.

I've never been with someone who made me feel this beautiful. This wanted. This secure.

Garrett certainly never came close, nor did any of the ones before him. I didn't know men like Rhodes existed. He's mature, he's confident, and he makes me feel like an absolute goddess.

We make plans for me to go back to Magnolia Row and stay with Sistine while he looks for a place for us to live, but the day before he's supposed to drive me back, I get a call from an unknown number.

I answer, and an older woman is on the other end.

"Micah Bonaventure?" she asks when I answer.

"Who is this?" I ask.

"Allette Aspley," she says with no further explanation, which is not needed anyway since I know exactly who she is. She and her husband are the two most prominent lawyers in Magnolia Row. They've had an office downtown for ages.

"Yes! Mrs. Aspley. How can I help you?"

"Honey, I should ask you the same thing. I've been waiting for you to call me."

"Why?"

"About your grandmama's will, of course. I heard a rumor your mama is living in her house, but the property belongs to you, honey."

"What? My mom showed me a will that left everything to her."

"She did? What was the date on it?"

"I don't remember."

"Okay, honey. Let me check on this. I'll call you back."

We hang up. Rhodes is in the shower, so I sit on the bed and wait for him to get out. When he walks out in nothing but a towel, it's all I can do to not get distracted and rip it off.

"What?" he asks with a sly grin, catching me staring.

I blush and shake my head. "I got a call from a lawyer in Magnolia Row. She seems to think Nana left everything to me."

He raises his eyebrows in surprise. "Well, this is good news."

"I told her about the will my mom showed us, but she said—"

And just like that, the phone rings again from the same number.

"Micah, it's Allette again. I called the courthouse, and your grandmama only ever had one will with probate. I wrote it and I can guarantee your mama ain't getting a dime or a blade of grass from the estate. I dare her to try to produce something else or challenge it. Barbara was very clear on how she wanted her estate handled. There's no way she left your mama a single red penny."

I feel an enormous weight lift from my body. "Thank you, Mrs. Aspley. I'll be in touch."

After I get off the phone, Rhodes and I talk and decide the best plan of action is to call the police. We'll let them handle getting my mom off the property as soon as possible, so she's not there when we return home. I honestly never want to see her ever again. She's never been a constructive part of my life, and she's made the entire process of grieving Nana exponentially worse by trying to take away everything I have left.

That's not what a mother does. That's what a monster does.

The Magnolia Row PD calls when we're south of Montgomery to let me know she was escorted off the property without incident, but she was upset about some of her things still being in the house. While I'm still on the phone with them, I get a barrage of texts from her. Most of them are about her clothes, shoes, and a computer, but sprinkled in are the expected degradations calling me a brat, ungrateful, horrible child, and even a delightful message saying she wished she'd aborted me.

Rhodes clenches his jaw as I read them to him from the passenger seat and shakes his head, and it's honestly the only appropriate response. There are no words for how low she's willing to go.

"You don't have to worry about her anymore," he finally says when there's a break in the phone dings. "Like Patsy told you, you have a tribe. You don't need anything else. None of the garbage she's saying has anything to do with you."

He's right. Those are her issues, not mine.

"I love you," I say, holding his hand.

"I love you too."

I can't get enough of saying it. No matter how my anxiety spikes or what I'm worrying about, every time he says he loves me, a sense of calm washes over my body and spirit. Everything will be okay as long as I have him by my side.

When we get home, I pack all my mother's things I can find and leave them in garbage bags by the mailbox. I text her to let her know they're there, and Rhodes stands on the front porch watching her when she pulls up to make sure she doesn't get further than the edge of the yard.

Once we're sure my mother isn't coming back, we check on the store. Luckily, it doesn't look like she so much as drove to Bonaventure Antiques, so that's one less thing to worry about. Rhodes goes online and orders security systems for both the house and the store in case she returns, but we end up not needing them. My mother never comes back to Magnolia Row, and Rhodes and I pick up the pieces of my grandmother's beautiful life and irreplaceable soul. Slowly, we begin to make a new home for ourselves, and I start to envision the life my nana wanted for me all along.

EPILOGUE

Micah

It's Christmas in Magnolia Row, which means it's almost been a year since Rhodes moved here, and I've never been happier. He set up an office in the guest room and he and I sleep in my old room. I keep Nana's room exactly as she left it. I know Rhodes and I would have more space if we moved to the master bedroom, but it doesn't feel right. Though I've almost gotten through my year of firsts without her, I still miss her so much I swear I hear her whisper to me when it's quiet.

Even so, life has continued to carry me along. I take joy in little things with Rhodes, like watching television together, going for walks, and stopping by the hotel job site to let him show me what's going on there. We've even made a few midnight trips to the old dilapidated house on the river to explore and relive the magical first kiss that set my soul alight and told me yes, he is my forever love.

Sometimes I worry he misses his life in Birmingham, but he assures me he's excited about our new chapter together. Over the summer, his son had an internship with a big law firm in the city, so he was able to use Rhodes' condo during that time. He even came to Magnolia Row one Sunday to meet me, and while it was a little strange at first, given he and I are relatively close in age, he was nothing but kind, gracious, and seemed genuinely happy for his dad.

The structural restoration of the hotel was completed in October, so a crew of eight men took the fountain out of my shop and returned it to its original home. We had to take the front doors off the hinges to get it out, but we managed. It shines in the old hotel lobby, and I know Nana looks down and smiles when she sees that a small piece of her is now part of the hotel's legacy.

The hotel is primed, painted, and decorated in time for Christmas. *Southern Living* magazine even did a story about the full restoration in their November issue, so the place is fully booked for a year before it has even opened its doors.

Wilhelmina Caxton, whom I met a few times after Rhodes moved to Magnolia Row, is not one to miss an opportunity to celebrate herself, so she's decided to throw a lavish Christmas party in the hotel's ballroom and invited all her friends from Fairhope as well as everyone who is anyone in Magnolia Row. Rhodes and I were of course invited, a) since he's the architect and b) since she's apparently been lusting after him since they met, which she does not even try to hide even when I'm around. I get the feeling she only invited me out of a sense of propriety, but I don't care. I'm so excited to see the hotel in its full glory I can put up with her for one night. Besides, I have nothing to worry about. Rhodes' heart is all mine.

For the party, I wear one-strap red dress with huge flowers on the neckline and shoulder. My arms are bare, which is new for me, but Rhodes insists I look ravishing. Patsy helps with my hair, and I must say when I look in my brand-new full-length mirror, I do look beautiful. Most importantly, I look happy.

Rhodes, of course, is the sexiest man in the room in his tux. His hair has a little more gray than it did when we met over a year ago, but it only serves to make him look more of a gentlemen, like he just stepped out of a Jane Austen novel. Every time I look at him, I get goosebumps. I can't believe he's mine.

The party is a blast, though thanks to the open bar, most of Magnolia Row is smashed. The entire police force is there offering free safe rides to anyone who isn't okay to drive. Kendall is there with Pierre, her movie-star-turned-novelist fiancé, and we have a great time dancing. Patsy and Sistine are absent—Patsy couldn't find a babysitter for her kids, and Sistine would rather die than get dressed up for a formal party—but even though we miss them, we still have a great time.

When we leave the party, instead of turning left to go home, Rhodes turns right and drives towards the old house on the river.

"We can't go there tonight," I tell Rhodes. "I'm in this dress. I'll never be able to climb the fence."

"I have a surprise for you," he says.

We pull up to the house, and the gate is open.

"How did you—" I start to ask, but he taps my hand gently.

"I'll explain when we get there."

We're able to drive through the weeds and park right at the foot of the stairs leading to the front door. Moonlight glints off the broken windows at the top of the belvedere, and when Rhodes helps me out of the car, he puts his coat over my shoulders so I won't be too cold. He holds my hand and helps me navigate the uneven steps, then leads me into the house. It's pitch black since we didn't bring any lights, but Rhodes tells me to stand still in the foyer, the exact spot where we had our first kiss, and retrieves a small lantern from behind the staircase and turns it on. He puts it on the floor beside me, then pulls some papers out of the coat pocket that I hadn't even noticed were there.

"What's this?" I ask.

"The deed to this house," he says.

"Are you serious?"

"One hundred percent. Turns out Pauline Cavendish owned it. She agreed to sell it to me for almost nothing after I told her I wanted to restore it for Barbara Bonaventure's granddaughter. I know you're attached to our home now, since it's where you grew up with your nana, but I thought maybe we could fix this place up and have a fresh start, if that's what you want. Or we can restore it for fun and use it as a wedding venue or something. Either way, it's special to us, and I want you to have it."

My mouth drops and tears roll down my cheeks. My imagination runs wild with all the potential lying dormant in these walls. My head is spinning and I have to remind myself to breathe as I stand here dumbfounded.

"This is the most amazing Christmas gift you could've given me," I say. "This will be the adventure of a lifetime! Oh, I have so many ideas." I clasp my hands together and look around as I talk, but before my thoughts get away from me, Rhodes puts his hands on my face and kisses me.

"I have one more surprise for you," he says.

Then, like Cary Grant in an Old Hollywood movie, he gets down on one knee and pulls a small box out of his pocket.

I gasp. I can barely see the ring in this light, but I don't even care what it looks like. This moment is everything.

"Micah, you've been the light of my life since we met. I love you, I love our life here together, and I want nothing more than for you to be my wife."

My heart explodes and my hands shake so much I have to grab him to keep steady. "Yes, yes, yes," I exclaim through happy tears. "A million times yes!"

He slides the ring on my finger, and he barely has time to stand before I grab him and kiss him as hard and with as much intensity as that night over one year ago in this very spot. And, just like then, I feel my body begin to float, my soul so happy not even gravity can keep my feet on the ground.

THE END

ACKNOWLEDGMENTS

This book's journey came during a tumultuous time in my life. I plotted *Just a Number* in early 2024 with no idea of what the year would bring. I knew it would be a story with a happily ever after ending, but having lost my grandmother the year before, I wanted to incorporate grief into the narrative and have my character navigate that process. Little did I know how prescient the subject of loss would be while bringing this book into the world. I was writing the first draft during the summer of 2024 when my husband's father passed away. Between finishing the draft and editing, my stepmother lost her long battle with cancer. Now, as I'm putting the final touches on this book in early 2025, I'm only a few days removed from my husband's mother's funeral. It's been a lot.

I decided to dedicate this book to my stepmother Lisa for a number of reasons. She had a radiant personality and always had a positive outlook. She was so excited to see me begin my writing career. I received the proof copies of my first book, *Wildest Dreams*, a few days before she passed away. Though she wasn't able to read it, I did get a chance to show it to her and she was overjoyed. I know she would have loved it had her body held on a little bit longer. She enjoyed a love story with a happy ending, and as a fierce and loyal friend herself, she would have adored the friendships in these books. Lisa, we miss you and know that you're looking down on us with a smile.

I'm blessed beyond words with people who have supported me and my work both directly and indirectly throughout the past year. Kista Hamilton and Wendy Wason both read an early rough draft of this story and provided invaluable feedback that helped me shape this book into the polished gem you now hold in your hands. Both of these ladies have proven to be absolute rocks in my life and always know what I need to hear when I need to hear it. I am further blessed by my friendships with Lauren Lamey and Stephanie Kelly, who have gone above and beyond for me and kept me sane while I worked on launching my new career.

Joining Southern Magic, my local Romance Writers of America chapter, was one of the best things I did last year. I've learned so much from this community of women and they continue to be an invaluable resource for me in this crazy industry. Everyone brings a unique perspective to the group and I'm so fortunate to call them my friends.

Furthermore, I can say without a doubt that this book would be a hot mess without the hard work of my editor, Karie Crawford. I'm beyond fortunate to have found someone who is not only a gifted editor, but who also really understands and appreciates my work. I've learned a lot about the craft from her and look forward to our continued work together on this series.

Those who follow me on social media have seen my grumpy Yorkie/cowriter, Piper. Piper has been my four-legged baby love for fifteen years and has brought immeasurable joy to my life. Sometimes it's hard to juggle both a dog and a computer in my lap while I write, but we make it work.

Most importantly, I want to thank my husband, Will, for everything. Absolutely everything. I can say in full confidence that this book would not have happened without him, nor would I have any writing career to speak of without his support. He is my biggest cheerleader, my greatest inspiration, and the love of my life. Thank you.

I'd also like to acknowledge anyone reading this who may be struggling with body image issues. I hope Micah was a relatable inspiration for you and served as a reminder that you are seen, you are valued, and you are deserving of love.

On a final note, I want to thank you, dear reader, for following me on this new adventure. So many people reached out with positive words and support after *Wildest Dreams* was released. Your kindness and encouragement mean more to me than you'll ever know.

ABOUT THE AUTHOR

Anna May grew up in rural Alabama and studied English at Auburn University. She lives in Birmingham with her husband and a grumpy Yorkie. She is the author of *Wildest Dreams: A Magnolia Row Novel*. *Just a Number* is her second book.

Be sure to visit annamaybooks.com and sign up for the Anna May newsletter to get more information about books, merchandise, and all things Magnolia Row!

instagram.com/annamaybooks